"You're safe now."

Jordan sat next to her and Courtney instantly felt the air charge around her. Attraction replaced fear. His arms opened to her and she embraced the invitation, burying her face in his masculine chest.

Memories flooded her as she breathed in his all-male, uniquely Jordan scent. It would be so easy to get lost in it and let him be her strength. There was a baby to think about now. She took in a breath meant to fortify her, but it only ushered in more of Jordan's scent.

Pulling on all the strength she had left, she moved away from him and hugged her knees to her chest. "I'm sorry about that. I won't make it a habit."

"Promise me that anytime you need someone to lean on you'll call me." There was so much honesty and purity in the words that she almost gave in.

WHAT SHE SAW

USA TODAY Bestselling Author
BARB HAN

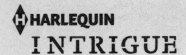

HARLEQUIN
INTRIGUE

All my love to Brandon, Jacob and Tori,
the three great loves of my life.

To Babe, my hero, for being my greatest love and
my place to call home.

And to book lovers like Amy McWilliams,
who I also get to call my friend.

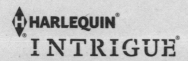

Recycling programs
for this product may
not exist in your area.

ISBN-13: 978-1-335-13654-1

What She Saw

Copyright © 2020 by Barb Han

This edition published by arrangement with Harlequin Books S.A.

For questions and comments about the quality of this book,
please contact us at CustomerService@Harlequin.com.

Harlequin Enterprises ULC
22 Adelaide St. West, 40th Floor
Toronto, Ontario M5H 4E3, Canada
www.Harlequin.com

Printed in U.S.A.

USA TODAY bestselling author **Barb Han** lives in north Texas with her very own hero-worthy husband, three beautiful children, a spunky golden retriever/standard poodle mix and too many books in her to-read pile. In her downtime, she plays video games and spends much of her time on or around a basketball court. She loves interacting with readers and is grateful for their support. You can reach her at barbhan.com.

Books by Barb Han

Harlequin Intrigue

Rushing Creek Crime Spree

Cornered at Christmas
Ransom at Christmas
Ambushed at Christmas
What She Did
What She Knew
What She Saw

Crisis: Cattle Barge

Sudden Setup
Endangered Heiress
Texas Grit
Kidnapped at Christmas
Murder and Mistletoe
Bulletproof Christmas

Cattlemen Crime Club

Stockyard Snatching
Delivering Justice
One Tough Texan
Texas-Sized Trouble
Texas Witness
Texas Showdown

Harlequin Intrigue Noir

Atomic Beauty

Visit the Author Profile page at Harlequin.com.

CAST OF CHARACTERS

Deputy Courtney Foster—After being shot in the line of duty, can she return to Jacobstown to find a safe haven?

Jordan Kent—He came home to handle the family ranching business and found out he's going to become a father, unless a serial killer has his way.

Gus Stanton—An accident cost him his livelihood and family, and gave him a lifelong limp. Is he angry enough to take his losses out on others?

Jason Millipede—Bullied as a kid, is he exacting revenge on a whole town?

Reggie Barstock—Reggie sightings are back. He's definitely a criminal and a creep, but has he graduated to murder?

Zach McWilliams—He took a chance hiring Courtney. Will her homecoming be tainted by a serial killer?

Chapter One

Deputy Courtney Foster sat at the oblong wooden conference table in the sheriff's office, clicking a pen. The distraction helped her focus on work and not the sick feeling swirling in her stomach, building, threatening to send her racing to the trash can. She'd skipped her usual early-morning cup of coffee in favor of salted crackers.

"I just got a call from the Meyers," her boss, Zach McWilliams, said on a frustrated-sounding sigh. "They've decided it's not safe in Jacobstown anymore. Trip Meyer made a point of telling me that he's afraid for his daughters to come home from the university over spring break."

"I'm sorry," Courtney offered.

Deputy Lopez shuffled into the room with coffee in hand and took a seat next her.

"Morning," he practically grumbled.

"Does 5:00 a.m. count as morning? Or is it still the night before?" She tried to lighten the heavy mood.

"Technically, I think it's still the night before," Lopez agreed.

Everyone was up early and taking extra shifts in order to ensure the town's safety.

"Do we know the exact timeline for when the small-animal killings began?" she asked Zach. He'd been working on the case with a volunteer. Lone Star Lonnie was also a close family friend and foreman of KR, Kent Ranch, one of the largest and wealthiest ranches in the state of Texas.

"We've been able to reach back as far as a year ago with the help of a forensic team out of Fort Worth," Zach responded.

The twisted psycho who had been dubbed the Jacobstown Hacker had begun killing small animals a year ago? The man had moved onto a heifer, butchering its left hoof and then leaving the poor animal to bleed out and die near Rushing Creek on the Kent Ranch.

There'd been more heifer killings after that, spaced out over weeks. It appeared that the twisted jerk had begun on small animals like rabbits and squirrels before moving on to bigger game. All the animals he'd butchered had been females, which had been a warning sign to all the women in town. And he graduated to killing a person—Breanna Griswold.

An investigation revealed that the twenty-seven-year-old victim had been in and out of group homes in Austin for the seven years of her life leading up to her last. She'd grown up in Jacobstown but had moved away during high school. Courtney remembered her from years ago. Breanna had moved back to town a couple of months before her murder.

She was a loner, known to sleep in random places around town when she was on a bender. She was murdered with the same MO as the animals —a severed left foot.

With Breanna's recent murder and the fact the killer was still on the loose, everyone seemed on edge. Courtney started working the clicker on the pen in double time.

"Do you mind?" Deputy Lopez motioned toward the noisemaker in her hand. Lopez was average height, in his mid-thirties and had dark hair and eyes. He was medium build and had a pronounced nose.

"Sorry." Courtney released the pen, and it tumbled onto the desk. Her unsettled stomach made all kinds of embarrassing sounds. For the second time this morning, Courtney thought she might throw up on the deputy who was seated next to her.

She was pretty certain that Lopez would not be amused. She'd been on the job a few weeks now and was still getting her bearings in the small, tight-knit sheriff's office. Coming home to Jacobstown was supposed to be a safe haven from her stressful job working for Dallas Police Department as a beat cop...

An involuntarily shiver rocked her as she thought about the past, about what had happened in Dallas.

"We're no closer to finding answers. Breanna deserves better from us." Zach tapped his knuckles on the table. Everyone knew the victim and her circumstances. Her only family, a mother and a brother, had walked away from her and moved to Austin years ago. Breanna had tracked them down there, but rumor had it she became homeless shortly after.

Her mother had a reputation for drinking and using physical violence on her children. Even so, every mother—even the bad ones—deserved justice for a murdered daughter. Breanna had been a grown woman who made her own mistakes, but people cared that she was gone. The horrific murder had rocked the bedroom community.

Another bout of nausea struck, and Courtney's breakfast threatened to make another appearance. She glanced up in time to see Zach staring at her.

"Everything okay?" he asked.

"I'll be fine." She could only hope this would pass soon. "I'm sure I ate something bad at the potluck yesterday. I should know better by now, but I can't resist beef and bean taco casserole."

"You're braver than I." Lopez cracked a smile,

breaking the tension. Courtney glanced at the scar on his neck. He'd taken a bullet trying to protect a mother and daughter a few months ago, when the quiet town had experienced its first crime wave since the Hacker began his work.

"I stick to vegetables and dessert. No one ever got sick from eating raw carrots," Lopez touted.

"No one ever enjoyed them, either." Courtney smiled, but it was weaker than she wanted it to be. She couldn't force it right now through another wave. Acid burned her throat, and it was taking all her energy to keep from losing it.

"Tasted fine to me." Lopez shrugged.

"We're short on solid leads." Zach steered the meeting back on track, and the mood immediately shifted to all business. Zach had mentioned that she'd be a good addition to his team when he hired her. The Jacobstown Hacker was all anyone could think about, he'd said. The town needed someone with big-city experience. People were getting anxious. Everyone was willing to pitch in to help, which created a whole different kind of chaos. A volunteer room had been set up in the office down the hallway, where folks volunteered to man the tip line.

The fact that people cared about each other was one of the many reasons Courtney had moved back to Jacobstown. She'd missed that small-town feel when she lived in a big city. The sheer volume of cases in Dallas caused law enforcement to focus most of its energy on high-priority cases. Whereas here at home, even the marginalized were cared for. People looked out for each other as best they could, and that included every resident. Even the ones who seemed intent on harming themselves.

Courtney had friends here. She'd been good friends with Zach's younger sister, Amy. She'd also been close to Amy's cousin Amber Kent at one time. But Courtney didn't want to think about the Kents. Especially not Jordan, who'd been two years ahead of her in school when they were all kids. He'd also ignored her for most of her life and teased her as teenagers. And then there were those few days at the cabin six weeks ago.

That week, great as it had been, was over. He'd gone back to Idaho and the property his family owned there, and she'd moved on to start her new job as a deputy for his cousin.

"Is there no one besides Reggie Barstock on our suspect list?" Courtney asked.

Zach shook his head.

"There have to be others," she continued.

"No one as strong as Reggie," Deputy Lopez said.

"Because he has a criminal record?" She didn't see how burglaries catapulted him into the category of serial killer. "How old is Reggie now?"

"Thirty-three." Zach clasped his hands and rested them on the conference table.

"I didn't know him very well growing up. He was quite a few years older than me, but I'm picturing someone with a higher IQ here. Am I alone?" From everything she knew about serial killers, they were intelligent, lacked a conscience but could be incredibly charming when it served them. At least, the ones who got away with their crimes were. And this perpetrator had the presence of mind to ensure he left no DNA behind. That took some calculating on his part.

The first heifer had been found near Rushing Creek, and the other animals had eventually been found near there. Breanna had been discovered two miles up the creek on the Kent family property. Courtney would have to speak to family members as part of the investigation. She figured it wouldn't be too difficult to bypass Jordan, since he lived out of state. The last thing she wanted to do was run into him again while she still felt so vulnerable after their fling.

"Do you have any other ideas for suspects?" Lopez leaned toward her.

"No. But the Jacobstown Hacker is careful, calculating. He's methodical," she continued. "I'm not completely convinced that I'm seeing that in Reggie's file."

"I feel the same way about Gus Stanton." Lopez

snapped his fingers. "He's been home on worker's comp after an accident a few years ago unloading his rig. He lives on the outskirts of town on a couple of acres. Keeps to himself mostly."

Having returned to town a month and a half ago, Courtney had to defer to Lopez and the sheriff for up-to-date information about residents. She hadn't heard of Gus Stanton growing up, so he must've moved to the area after she'd left.

"Why don't you go out and check on him? See if you can get a feel for his emotional state," Zach said. "If he has a bad left foot from the accident, I want to know about it."

"Does Gus have a family?" Courtney asked. The guy she was looking for was a loner.

"He's divorced with two kids. I believe his ex moved the kids to New Braunfels to be with her folks a couple of years back," Zach supplied.

"Sounds like we've doubled our list of suspects," Courtney said. There were half a dozen names that had been submitted and cleared almost immediately. The pair of suspects they had didn't exactly fit the loose profile they'd developed. It was impossible not to feel like they were letting the community down.

All the townsfolk were antsy, sitting on pins and needles in anticipation of another strike. People had taken to locking their doors and looking at their neighbors twice. Tips were coming in, but most people were on the wrong track. Every kid who'd ever thrown a rock in the wrong place at the wrong time had been named as a possible lead.

Zach leaned back in his chair and pinched the bridge of his nose as though to stem a headache. "Since Lopez is taking Gus, why don't you interview Reggie's former teachers, friends, neighbors. See what you can come up with about what kind of student he was. If he's smarter than we're giving him credit for, I want to know that, too."

"Will do, Zach." It was habit to call him by his first name after growing up friends with his sister, and yet it felt awkward after the formality of working in a big-city department.

Courtney picked up the pen and started clicking it again. She caught herself this time and set the pen down. She stretched her long, lean fingers over it.

"Go see what you can find out, and we'll meet again tomorrow." Zach glanced up at the whiteboard on the adjacent wall, where there were two names.

"Have there been any new Reggie sightings?" Courtney stood up, got hit with another wave and had to plant a hand on the table in order to steady herself.

"You sure you're okay to work?" Zach's brow creased with concern.

"I'm good," she responded a little too quickly. "No more potluck for me."

"To answer your question, yes. There's a new sighting almost every day. Nothing has panned out so far," Zach said.

Getting out of the stuffy office where she could grab some fresh air was her top priority. The department-issue SUV assigned to her was at the opposite end of the parking lot.

Taking in a lungful of crisp late-morning air, she was reminded how good it felt just to breathe. She'd taken a new job in a new city—not technically new, but she hadn't lived in Jacobstown in almost a decade—and this was supposed to be a fresh start after what had happened in Dallas when a protest turned into civil unrest. Eight officers had been killed that day, three of whom she'd been very close to. One of whom she'd been intimate with.

Courtney had barely escaped with her life. She'd gone back to the job after a three-month recovery and counseling stint after being shot. But living in the city, doing that job had lost its appeal. Since law enforcement was all she knew and at one time had been her passion, she'd called Zach and asked if she could come work for him.

The rest, as they said, was history. Courtney climbed up and slid behind the wheel of her SUV. Her white-knuckle grip did little to calm her churning stomach. She already knew a few teachers she wanted to speak to, and Zach had said he'd have his secretary, Ellen Haiden, send over their home addresses. School was still in session, and only one of Reggie's teachers had retired in the last decade.

But Courtney had something to do first.

The drive to the big-box store in Bexford took a solid forty-five minutes from the office. She could only pray she wouldn't recognize anyone once she got inside.

Courtney parked her vehicle off to the side of the building and took the walk to the front door while fighting against the urge to vomit. She walked past the row of neatly stacked carts. She didn't need one but didn't exactly want to hold a pregnancy test out in the open, either. She picked up a handbasket instead, figuring she could load it with a few items.

Part of the reason she'd come to this store was the fact that it had self-checkout stands. That and the point that she didn't want the whole town of Jacobstown to know she thought she might be pregnant. If she was, then, yes, she would have to have an awkward conversation with the baby's father, but she'd rather not deal with the gossip if she turned out to be stressing over being late on her cycle for no reason.

Walking through the aisle caused her pulse to race. A man walked past. She froze, pretending to be interested in a feminine napkin package. She mentally chided herself for being ridiculous. But this felt so much bigger than she could handle. If word got out, there'd be questions, and there was no way she wanted this tidbit getting around.

Her heart played a steady beat, hammering her rib cage.

It was then she realized she should've bought the other items first so she could immediately cover what she came for.

Taking in another deep breath brought enough calm over her to pick up the pregnancy test and drop it into her basket. She moved over two aisles and randomly threw in any item that she might ever need. Allergy pills. Stomach acid reducer. Cotton balls.

It shouldn't be a big deal to get from where she stood in the middle of the store, and yet it felt like miles away.

She turned and out of the corner of her eye caught sight of a youngish man who favored his left leg when he walked. The hairs on the back of her neck pricked. She told herself that her reaction was most likely because of the conversation she'd had with Zach and Lopez a little while ago and not because the Jacobstown Hacker was in The Mart walking twenty feet in front of her.

His back was to her, but she could see that he was average height and build, maybe even a little wiry. She'd learned the hard way that wiry guys could be surprisingly strong. His hair was light brown in a short cut, commonly referred to as a buzz. He wore Carolina-blue basketball shorts and a dark hoodie.

There were all kinds of logical reasons that could account for his slight limp, Courtney reminded herself as she kept one eye trained on him. He turned at the end of the aisle toward the sporting goods section. This guy could be coming from the gym. He could have strained a muscle in a workout. Or he might play sports and could have tweaked his ankle during a game. It could've been a pickup game. How many of her colleagues in Dallas had done the same during last-minute lunch-hour basketball rounds?

She was being paranoid, but with no answers in Breanna's murder after weeks of investigating, everyone with a limp was worth checking out. The reality that the killer knew the area struck. He really could be any guy she'd just walked past in order to follow Blue Trunks. Ice-cold creepy-crawlies trailed up and down her spine when she really thought about it. A familiar shot of adrenaline jacked her heart rate up a few notches. She used to get a burst of excitement when that happened. Now, it felt a lot like dread as she reminded herself to control her breathing. Her stress response was out of whack after what had happened on her last job.

Courtney increased her speed as she rounded

the aisle. She ran smack into a hard, male chest that felt more like a wall.

Before she could tell the man to watch where he was going, she blinked up. Jordan Kent.

"What are you doing here?" The words flew out, and her cheeks flamed with embarrassment. If he saw the pregnancy test in her basket...

No, he could not see that. She subtly shifted her elbow backward in order to use her body to block the contents in the basket. Her skin still sizzled from the weeklong fling they'd had a month and a half ago.

The tall, over-the-top handsome rancher took a step back. His dark curls were barely contained underneath a black Stetson. A slow grin spread across perfect lips and straight white teeth in one of those smiles that had been so good at seducing her. He had the sexiest dimple on his right cheek. He was one seriously irresistible, hot package. Another bout of nausea struck. She didn't want to be reminded of exactly how tempting he'd been.

Jordan quirked a dark brow. "Shopping. Why? Is it against the law now?"

COURTNEY STARED AT Jordan like he had two foreheads. He'd been used to teasing her when they were kids but running into her in the least likely place a month and a half ago, he'd seen her in a whole new light.

"Why aren't you still in Idaho?" She blinked at him like he might be a mirage or something.

"Family business. I was asked to come home." The last time he'd seen Courtney ten years ago, she'd been the cute but young friend of his little sister. Running into her after a decade of absence had caused him to see that she'd grown into an intelligent, strong and beautiful woman. An attraction like wildfire had spread through both of them, and they'd been consumed by the flames for a solid seven days and nights.

But their time together wasn't all incredible sex and lighthearted teasing. She woke in the middle of the night many times shaking and crying. He'd comforted her until she fell back asleep. When he'd tried to sit her down and talk about it on the seventh day, she'd made it clear that she had a job to begin and a new life that didn't involve him.

He'd thought about her more times than he cared to admit in the past thirty-seven days. Her quick wit. Her soft curves. Those pink lips.

Hell, he had no business appreciating those anymore. She'd been real clear on where they stood. It was most likely his bruised ego that had him thinking about her more than he knew better than to allow. Usually he was the one walking out, not the other way around.

"What's wrong?" he asked as she tried to look around his shoulder. Did she have a boyfriend?

The only thing he'd known for certain about her during their fling was that she wasn't married. He should've asked about a relationship but assumed she wouldn't have spent the week in bed with him if she'd been dating someone else.

He'd also thought about that haunted look in her eyes when she first woke from a nightmare. That, he might never forget.

She was almost a foot shorter than his six feet three inches. She had to come in at five feet six, maybe seven. Her shiny auburn hair was pulled back in a low ponytail. She had just enough curves to be a real woman, and his fingers itched to get lost on that silky skin of hers again.

"Sorry. I was just watching someone, and…" Her face twisted, and she took a step to the right in order to get a clear view of the person.

Jordan had never felt awkward with a woman before. Normally, he spent time with people who didn't expect much in return. After a few rounds of hot sex and mutual enjoyment, they'd part ways. Neither side tried to drag out the fling or make a big deal out of walking away.

He told himself that he felt a pang of jealousy with a strong dose of heartache seeing her again because he knew Courtney, but that wasn't completely true. He couldn't put his finger on exactly why this felt different from the many others he'd spent time with. It just did.

"Well, I should get out of your way, deputy," he said to her. Her cheeks flushed, and her tongue darted across full pink lips. Jordan ignored the warning shot to his chest.

It didn't matter. Courtney seemed to have no interest in him. But the week he'd spent with her had felt like a homecoming. Not since he'd lost his parents—and maybe even long before then—had Jordan felt like he belonged somewhere. Sure, he and his five siblings had taken over the family ranching business along with associated mineral rights. Their inheritance was spread across three states, with significant holdings in Texas.

No one in his family needed to work another day for a paycheck. They got up at 4:00 a.m. to face a long day of work because ranching was in their blood and they loved the land. Jordan was no different. But the ranch didn't feel like home to him anymore.

He stepped aside.

Courtney grabbed his arm and motioned for him to scoot back over.

Well, he really was confused now. "What's going on, Courtney?"

"I'm sorry. I was watching a possible suspect." She glanced at Jordan, and those eyes with cinnamon-colored flecks sent a bolt of lightning straight to his heart. He needed to develop a thicker skin when it came to her, because right then he wanted to haul her against his chest and welcome her back home properly. But that ship had sailed when she'd refused to speak to him again.

Damned if she wasn't distracted now. Sure, his ego took a hit. Most women made themselves a little too available for the youngest and only single Kent brother.

He told himself that was the reason he felt a sting in his chest and not because he had stronger feelings for Courtney.

"Don't let me stand in the way of your job." Hadn't those been the words he'd used when she'd told him that their time together had been special, but she needed to focus on her work at his cousin's office?

"I'm sorry, Jordan. It's a case I'm working on. It's getting inside my head a little bit," she said by way of apology. "I should go."

Courtney turned toward the front of the store. He should've walked away right then and there. It was his fool pride that had him standing his ground like it didn't matter. His bruised ego wanted to say otherwise, but that's all it was.

Jordan glanced down, and then he saw something in her basket that gave him pause.

Was this the reason she'd rejected him?

Evidence that she had been in another relationship stared back at him.

Chapter Two

Courtney issued another apology before ducking down the nearest aisle in order to put as much distance between her and Jordan as possible. She could only pray that he hadn't seen the contents of her basket.

Blue Trunks had disappeared. She searched aisle after aisle with no luck. Biting back her frustration and shock at seeing Jordan in Texas again, Courtney used the self-checkout machine and stalked toward her SUV. Her situation was bad enough without running into Jordan.

As she tossed the bag onto the passenger seat, she saw Blue Trunks moving through cars.

She closed the door to her SUV and hit the auto lock on her key ring. She stuffed the keys inside her pocket before resting her hand on the butt of her weapon. The sun was high in the sky, and it was cold enough to require a coat. She wore a deputy jacket, which essentially was like a billboard.

She didn't mind as she doubled her stride so that she could get a look at Blue Trunks's face.

He stopped at his vehicle, an older-model pickup, which was not uncommon in these parts. He glanced around, and her blood chilled. She was still too far away to make out the details of his face.

"Excuse me, sir," she shouted, but his head dipped, disappearing before he acknowledged her.

She might not have been close enough to get a description of the color of his eyes, but he'd heard her. She'd bet money on the fact. Didn't that send another chill racing up her spine?

It meant he was guilty of something. The pickup jutted forward as she got closer, and then it disappeared before she could get a look at the plate. There were enough cars moving in and out of the busy lot to block her view.

Running to catch up to Blue Trunks caused her to be winded, which wasn't normally a problem for her. She'd been athletic growing up and had easily passed the department's physical fitness requirements, a stumbling block for many applicants. She woke every morning at 5:00 a.m. to run. It was a habit she'd picked up after playing high school sports.

Courtney's mother had disappeared with her baby brother when Courtney was ten years old. Her brother, Cord, had been supposed to start kindergarten that year. With a mother who could walk away from a ten-year-old child and a father who had no problem with lengthy punishments, what chance did Courtney have at being a decent parent? She'd asked her ob-gyn to shut off the possibility of parenthood permanently, but he'd said she was too young to make a lifelong commitment to that decision. Courtney had other ideas. A wave of panic washed over her, and she needed to talk herself down as she realized her hands were shaking.

A wave of panic slammed into Courtney at the thought of being pregnant. What if parenting skills were inherited?

There was a strong possibility that she wasn't, she reminded herself. As she turned to make the walk back to her vehicle, she chewed on a few facts. She and Jordan had used protection every single time. She would've been on the pill except that it had been a waste of money after the cop she'd been dating seriously enough to have sex with had been killed practically in front of her eyes. Since sex had been the last thing on her mind when thinking about returning to her childhood hometown, she hadn't bothered to get a new prescription. Plus, she would be changing doctors once she got settled.

A wave of nausea struck like a physical blow. She pushed through and kept walking.

Back at her vehicle, Courtney opened the pas-

senger door and held on for dear life. She took
in a few deep breaths, reminding herself to blow
them out her nose slowly in order to calm her racing heart and churning stomach.

The overwhelming feeling of panic crushed her
ribs.

"Are you all right?" She'd recognize Jordan's
voice anywhere. It had that deep timbre that
wrapped around her. That man could make reading the ingredients of a soup can sound sexy.

"Yeah. Got a hold of something at a potluck that
isn't agreeing with me." She tried to wave him off.

"Can I get you some water?" There was genu-
ine concern in his tone, and it caused her heart to
squeeze.

As much as she didn't want to come off as a
jerk, she couldn't afford to let him stick around.
Especially with the way her body reacted when
he was close. Muscle memory had her wanting to
feel his hands on her, rough from working outside.
For having such rough hands, his touch had been
surprisingly soft. And those were more things she
couldn't afford to think about.

The pregnancy test should be safely tucked inside the bag, but she'd tossed that onto the passenger seat before she'd turned away. She didn't want
Jordan seeing something he shouldn't or asking
questions she didn't have answers to.

Courtney took in a deep, fortifying breath. "I'm okay. Thanks for offering, though."

A stomach cramp doubled her over. She turned away in time to empty the contents onto the parking lot. So much for being fine.

The next thing she knew, Jordan was next to her, comforting her. His hand on her back caused a whole different kind of reaction in her body. One that was totally out of place under the circumstances.

"That must've been some potluck," he commented.

She didn't respond.

"I saw the test in your basket, Courtney," he said flatly. "Are you pregnant?"

COURTNEY STOPPED THROWING UP. Jordan expected a response to his question. He waited. Because if she was pregnant, that meant she'd been in a relationship with someone else during their brief fling. Jordan might have the reputation of a playboy, but there were lines he never crossed and that was one of them. "Courtney—"

She stood up straight and stepped away from him.

"Take this." He handed her a bottle of water, which she took and then used to rinse out her mouth.

"Are you planning to answer me?" This whole

scenario was off. He couldn't imagine she would use him to cheat on someone else. He didn't normally misread people or their intentions.

Courtney locked gazes with him. "If I knew the answer to your question, I wouldn't need the test, now would I?"

"Why didn't you say something about being in a relationship?" he pressed.

She issued a grunt and twisted up her face with a *how dare you* look. She was offended?

"Is that what you think? I could—" she made eyes at him "—with *you* while two-timing my real boyfriend?"

Jordan started to speak but was cut off.

"Because if that's the kind of person you think I am, this conversation is over."

What exactly was she saying?

Jordan had to stop a second to let her words sink in. The gears in his head started grinding. The realization struck him like lightning on a sunny day, fast and out of the blue. *He* was the father. *If she was pregnant*, a struggling little voice in the back of his mind called out.

"If you'll excuse me, I have a murder investigation to get back to." She walked past him, and her shoulder bumped him as she passed by on her way to the driver's side of her vehicle.

Ignoring the intentional snub and the rockets of electricity from contact, he turned and caught her by the elbow. "Hold on. You're not getting away that easy."

"Neither one of us is if the test comes back positive," she retorted.

"I didn't ask for the easy road, but I deserve to know the outcome as much as you do." He held his ground. He got it—Courtney was scared, and she didn't do weak. The brave front she put up could be equated to a bull in a china shop, but she seemed to be clinging to hope, so he didn't call her out on it. He could tell that she was forcing her strength by the way her chin jutted out. Knowing her since they were kids had its advantages—being able to read her was one of them. And even though she'd annoyed him in his teen years, he'd noticed quite a few of her little quirks. They'd been damn adorable then—a fact he hadn't wanted to acknowledge in high school—and had turned straight-up sexy as an adult.

He almost laughed out loud. Courtney Foster would balk at being described as adorable.

The tension in her shoulders released like a balloon letting out air. Now it made sense why she was out here shopping on the outskirts of town when there were plenty of stores in Jacobstown. She didn't want to take the chance that anyone would see her buying a pregnancy test. He got it. Everyone in town knew each other, and people talked. Having a baby would be a big story. The news that Courtney Foster had come home after living in Dallas for the past decade had just died down after a month of hitting the gossip rounds, according to his sister Amber. She'd said there'd been talk for weeks. It was a main topic of conversation and had given the townsfolk a break from chewing on the other big news in Jacobstown—the Hacker and the possibility he would strike again soon.

"I have one stop to make, and then I'm on my lunch break. You can come if you want. It was never my intention to hide anything from you, Jordan. There might not even be anything to discuss." The hope in her voice at the end of her sentence made him realize this had taken her by surprise as much it had him.

"We were careful," he reassured. "It'll be fine."

"It was probably the potluck," she added, and the hopefulness in her voice struck him again.

"I'll bring my truck around to follow you." He didn't know where she lived. After their tryst, he'd gone back to Idaho. This was his first time back to Jacobstown since.

"What kind of family business brings you to town, anyway?" she asked.

"I already told you. Family business."

She used the contents of the water bottle to wash the concrete instead of pressing for a better answer.

A few minutes later, he was behind her on the road.

Jordan hadn't given much thought to becoming a father. His brothers and sister had all found happiness in the past few years with children and spouses. The Kent brood as a whole had grown exponentially, and that was good for them.

Fatherhood was not a job that Jordan had ever craved. If Courtney was pregnant, there was no doubt that he'd do the right thing by her, by his child. But that didn't mean he had to be in a relationship with Courtney to be there for his child.

They could start as friends, because they'd need common ground in order to co-parent.

And that's where Jordan stopped himself. Co-parenting and babies and entanglements weren't on the schedule for him. Besides, the two of them had been careful to use a condom every time. This was probably nothing more than a scare.

Half an hour later, Courtney pulled up in front of a small ranch-style house with crisscross wire fencing.

His eyebrow shot up as she approached his vehicle.

"Do you mind waiting for me at the gas station a block away?" she asked.

"No problem." He forced his gaze away from her sweet backside as she walked toward the home's front door. He pulled away thinking that he was probably seeing things, but he could've

sworn she had a different look, a glow. And maybe
a few more curves that looked damn good on her,
but he reminded himself how easy it had been for
her to shut down any budding feelings and force
him out of her life.

That was the last kind of person he needed to be
around. Damn, if she was pregnant, both of their
lives were going to change. He thought about the
baby boom happening at the ranch. The fact that
he couldn't stick around too long in one place without going a little crazy. He loved his nieces and
nephews. But he'd always been the outsider in the
family. He'd always chosen the lone path of living
far away from Jacobstown, out of Texas.

True to Courtney's word, she didn't take long.
She didn't circle back to talk this time as she pulled
up beside him. She navigated onto the two-lane
highway that led to Jacobstown. He could only
assume they were heading to her house. Jordan
had no idea where she lived. They'd stayed at her
uncle's abandoned fishing cabin, and then he'd left
town at the end of the week.

A baby? What in hell's name had they done to
their lives?

Jordan pulled in behind her at a small bungalow-
style house on Acorn Street. She parked and then
motioned for him to follow her inside. The place
sat on what looked to be a quarter of an acre, in his
best estimation. The house was made of white sid-

ing and had wood shutters. There were decorative flower pots on a small porch. It looked like something out of one of those home-decorating shows. Jordan had been subject to a few episodes while dining at small eateries on the road back and forth from Texas to Idaho.

Reality was a gut punch as he caught sight of the bag in Courtney's hand.

In a few minutes, he'd learn if he was a father. He couldn't even contemplate the ways in which his life would change. He stopped her at the door before she opened it.

A question had been churning over and over in his mind on the ride over.

"Was there even a potluck?"

Chapter Three

"Technically, yes. But, no, I didn't eat anything," Courtney admitted. Ever since she'd gotten food poisoning her rookie year at her department's potluck, she'd skipped the line. She always brought her own food. She'd been so sick that she didn't even risk eating raw vegetables. That's how freaked out she was by them.

The best way to avoid eating the food without raising any eyebrows was to get a plate, excuse herself from line by saying she needed to take a call and then put her own food on the plate before returning to her table.

Later, she'd go along with saying Tony's meatballs were perfection and Angela's pasta melted in her mouth. She couldn't think about work without thinking about her old crew. The memory of her dead coworkers crashed down hard on her, squeezing air out of her lungs. The scene. The mob. The blood.

She looked up at Jordan, who'd gone sheet white. "Let's get this over with."

He nodded. His sunglasses hooded his eyes, and his expression was impossible for her to read. He'd been clear about never wanting kids even when they were young. She hoped that she wasn't about to cause his hopes and dreams to crash down around him.

"If it makes you feel any better, I'm totally freaked out by the remote possibility of having a baby," she said, pushing the door open. She didn't bother to check his reaction. He seemed pretty freaked out by how much his life might change. She'd just started a new job. Jacobstown was supposed to be a fresh start for her. A baby was nowhere in the plans. Besides, she wasn't in the right emotional place to bring a life into this world.

But if that's what she was dealing with, she needed to know now.

"Make yourself comfortable," she said to Jordan. He'd removed his hat and sunglasses, and he was pretty damn devastating-looking standing in her living room.

His white-knuckle grip on his hat belied his calm exterior.

He shot her a look that said her comment didn't make him feel any better. "What do you need to do?"

"I take this into the bathroom with me, do what I have to and then we wait." She held up the plastic bag in her hand.

"May as well put all this behind us," he said.

Courtney couldn't agree more. She peeled off her jacket and then disappeared down the hall. She returned a minute later holding the white stick that had the power to change both of their lives forever. She placed it on her coffee table on top of a magazine and stared at the little window. "Two lines will show up in there if I'm pregnant."

If Courtney hadn't already thrown up the contents of her stomach, she would be now.

Three minutes had never taken so long. Neither spoke. Then the stick test yielded a positive reading.

Jordan took a few steps toward the front window and stared out it. If he was waiting for her to speak, he'd be waiting one hell of a long time, because there were no words for what she was currently feeling.

She feared that he might be concocting a plan to ask her to marry him. "You don't have to do that, you know."

"What?" He finally found his voice after a few beats of silence.

"Propose." Her heart squeezed, which made it a total traitor. Courtney had no plans to get married. Especially not because she'd gotten pregnant. That hadn't worked out so well for her parents. Being in a loveless marriage had to be the worst sentence, and she understood why her mother had taken off when Courtney was barely ten years old. What she could never understand was why the woman took Courtney's baby brother but not her.

And she'd never know, because her mother and brother had died in a car crash on a Texas highway a month later. She'd never had the chance to ask why her own mother didn't love her enough to take her away from the father who'd abused all of them.

"I wasn't going to." Jordan raked his fingers through his hair. He turned around to face her, and his expression was granite. The sharp angles and hard planes made for one seriously gorgeous man. But he gave away nothing of what he was thinking.

He was a Kent, and that name meant something. Her family might've been a hot mess, but there was honor in being a Kent.

"This is a lot to take in all at once," she said, unable to read his thoughts.

"It's simple to me. I have every intention of stepping up to be a father, Courtney. You should know that off the bat," he started.

She tried to interrupt him, but he brought his hand up to shush her.

"Looks like both of us are thrown off by the news, but that doesn't change the fact that a baby is coming, and it deserves the best from both of us." She couldn't agree more about that part, and when she regained her bearings she figured that she would be saying the same thing. It was foreign to her to hear that from the opposite sex, but then, she'd never been in this situation with her boyfriend and fellow officer Bradley Decks. He'd had a nine-year-old son from a marriage that had ended badly, a boy he never saw. Decks had no plans to marry or have more children. That had most likely been the cause of her initial attraction to him when she really thought about it. He'd been safe.

"I never thought about becoming a mother," she admitted in a moment of weakness. "I mean, I never thought it was a job I'd ever want."

The expression Jordan wore told her that he felt the same way about fatherhood. "But here we are."

"Are you saying that you're not upset that having this baby is the only option for me?" she asked.

"Did I mention anything about that?" he asked, and she saw the first crack in his calm facade. Good—that meant he wouldn't try to pressure her into doing something she couldn't. For a brief second, she thought about adoption. But she'd always worry if her child was being treated the way she'd been.

"No." She'd just put a down payment on a new car. The house was a rental, and she didn't exactly have stores of money in the bank after using her personal savings to set up a college fund for her former boyfriend's kid before her move to Jacobstown. It only seemed the right thing to do considering Becks had lost his life on the job. Babies cost money. This unexpected turn of events definitely threw a wrench in her future plans.

"Good. Because we got into this situation together, and I'll see it through with you." The out-of-the-blue news had clearly caught them both off guard. She had no idea what that meant, but the determination in his eyes had her reaching for her purse.

"I have to get back to work," she said.

"No, you don't. Not after dropping that bomb. You don't get to run away so fast this time."

JORDAN PACED IN Courtney's living room. The place was cozy and had just enough feminine touches to make it feel homey. The warm-toned twin sofas faced each other in the main living area. The fabric looked like the kind he could sink into. A glass coffee table with a stack of novels, a magazine that was now in the trash and a vase with fresh flowers anchored the seating area.

There was a table for two in the dining area. He couldn't see the kitchen from where he stood. His world had tipped on its axis, and he was noticing her furniture? Damn, Jordan was losing it.

Courtney excused herself and came back with a glass of water. "I'd ask if you want something to drink, but you won't be staying long enough."

"You should eat." He stared at the glass in her hand.

"I don't need someone looking over my shoulder, Jordan. Say what you need to get off your chest and then go."

"Are you really this hardheaded or just mean-spirited?" He regretted those words as soon as he heard them come out of his mouth. Chalk that up to his impulsive nature.

"You remember where the door is, don't you?" Fire shot from her gaze, and he could almost see her temper rising.

Maybe this wasn't the best time to try to sort this out, heat of the moment being what it was. The news was too fresh. The shock too great.

"I spoke before I thought," he offered by way of an apology. Jordan was no good at those. He was even worse at talking to someone who'd made it clear she had no use for him in her life, but that didn't stop him from digging his heels in anyway.

"Yeah?" was all she said.

"You made it clear a few weeks ago that you didn't want or need anyone in your life," he started.

"Well, it's too late for me to continue thinking that now." She touched her belly, and he wondered if she realized she did it.

"Like it or not, I'm going to be in your life, too." That point needed to be made. He needed to be very clear. Surprise pregnancy or not, Jordan Kent didn't walk away from his flesh and blood.

She drew in a deep breath, making it very clear that she was tolerating him at this point. If they were going to be successful with a child, they needed to learn to work together.

"It's important that we establish some ground rules—"

"Is that right, Jordan? Do tell what you have in mind." Her nostrils flared.

"Settle down. I'm not trying to make this more difficult than it already is. If you haven't noticed, I'm attempting to do just the opposite." He used the same tone when he came across a spooked mare in the stable.

"You're right," she conceded. "It's a little difficult to start negotiating with you when I don't have the first idea of how I'm going to handle any of this." She still fumed, but he appreciated her honesty.

Normally, he'd push his point until he won. This was different. He didn't want to make Courtney more upset, especially in her condition. He was concerned about the nightmares she'd been having, too.

"Do you want to sit down and talk?" He never could get her to talk about herself, her past. Courtney's quick wit and their history made for long conversations. But he'd taken note of how she wormed her way out of any conversation that got too personal. It was just as well, considering neither one had wanted to be tethered by a serious relationship. Besides, they'd been together a week after not knowing each other for a decade. She'd changed. He'd changed. Life was much bigger than what happened in high school.

"Not really. I mean, I don't know what to say right now, and I have an ongoing murder investigation that needs my full—"

"Can you ask to be removed from the case?" Zach wouldn't keep her on it if he knew she was pregnant anyway. Speaking of family, he had a feeling that Amber was going to flip out when she heard the news.

"No." That sounded final. She offered no follow-up explanation.

"When do you plan to tell your boss about the baby?" Jordan asked. The minute Zach learned she was pregnant, he would put her on a desk for precaution. There was no way Zach would want her chasing down the Jacobstown Hacker with nausea threatening every few seconds. When she'd mentioned a murder investigation earlier, he'd known exactly which one.

"I haven't given it any thought, Jordan. Please don't tell anyone until we figure this out," she pleaded.

It wasn't a smart idea.

"Can you take a few days off? Call in sick?" he asked.

"I just started last month. How will that look?" She folded her arms, and he could see the wall coming up between them. He'd seen it before.

They'd have a round of the best sex of his life—
and, his ego hoped, hers—and then while still
tangled in the sheets, they'd talk into the early
morning hours. She'd settle into the crook of his
arm, and he'd hold her. They'd laugh about the
past, about how two years of age difference at fifteen and seventeen had seemed like so much but
how little it mattered now in their late twenties
and early thirties. Conversation would inevitably
move to her past or family, and she'd put up that
same wall. The one she'd erected now. The one
that shut down any meaningful progress.

Since this conversation had taken a wrong turn
down a bad path, he needed to step away.

"You know what?" His frustration made that
question come out harsher than he'd intended.

She didn't answer, probably couldn't see over
the wall. If she didn't want to try, why should he
make her?

"I'm not doing this. You seem determined to
figure this out on your own, so I'm done." Walking
out that door made him feel like the biggest jerk
in the world. All momentum stopped the minute
he sat inside his vehicle and he was suddenly unable to drive away.

Courtney was struggling. He could see it on the
concern lines of her forehead. She was standing in
quicksand. Amber had mentioned recently while
making small talk while waiting for the others

to join them on a conference call what had happened to Courtney in Dallas. Jordan had looked up the massacre. The attack on officers had been brutal. The organizers of the peaceful protest had no connection, no idea what was about to happen. The bloodshed. The officers. The scene out of a horror show.

It explained the nightmares.

He'd heard gossip about an abusive father in town years ago. There'd been so much disdain in the voices as they recounted his acts of violence. The beatings became so bad the summer before Courtney's senior year that a neighbor had heard about them and finally stepped in. Amber and Amy had been distraught because they'd been friends with Courtney. She'd never let on about what was happening at home.

Courtney's father had been arrested. She'd been taken into the foster care system until she turned eighteen, which had been ten months later. And then, as far as Jordan knew, Mr. Foster had died a couple of years after that.

At the same time, Jordan had been in his own world, a sophomore at the University of Texas. He'd dropped out that summer and moved to Idaho, where he'd stayed all these years.

Coming home to Jacobstown when his mother had died and then not too long after his father followed in her footsteps had been foreign. But then, he'd always been the kind of person who needed to make his own way in life.

Jordan Kent relied on no one. And preferred it that way. So, why hadn't he started his engine and pulled away yet?

Jordan bit out a string of curses before pushing open the driver's side door and getting out of the cab of his pickup.

He stood there in the cold for a long time, staring at the bungalow.

And then the front door opened. Courtney stood there with her balled fist on her right hip.

"You stand out there on my lawn any longer and you'll freeze to death."

Chapter Four

"I'm sorry." Jordan hoped those two heartfelt words were enough.

"You want coffee?" Courtney opened the door a little wider and walked away.

"Is that a good idea for you?" He had no idea what the rules were for a pregnant woman, but coffee only upset his stomach when he was already nauseous.

"Probably not. It's not for me," she said. "I'm having water, and we'll see if I keep that down."

"Coffee sounds good." He closed the door behind him and took off his hat.

"Have a seat." She motioned toward the table.

Jordan took her up on the offer, figuring a little goodwill on his part would go a long way toward figuring out what their next steps were going to be.

A few minutes later, she joined him at the table and handed over a fresh cup of steaming brew. He thanked her and took the first sip, enjoying the burn on his throat.

"What family business has you back in town?" she asked.

"Everyone's concerned about the Hacker. I came so we'd have extra eyes around the ranch." He denied the part of him that said he'd hoped to run into her again.

The reason for his timing seemed to dawn on her as she rocked her head. "Right. Breanna was found at Rushing Creek as were the heifers."

"There was no sign of struggle, and the jerk got past increased security, which doesn't sit well." Jordan took another sip as guilt took a shot at him. He felt the blow square in his chest. That old, familiar voice resurfaced. He should've stuck around when he was home a few weeks ago. He might've been the difference. Now, because of his absence, a woman had been killed on the family's property, land that was sacred to them.

"You guys own so much acreage. It would be impossible to cover every inch with a person— or a camera, for that matter. The creek itself is how long?" Some of her color was returning to her cheeks. With her hair pulled off her face she was even more beautiful than he remembered, and that realization caused a second shot to his chest.

"Twenty-seven miles," he supplied.

"I spent so many summers playing around that

creek. I hate what happened there, and I can only imagine what Breanna's family has been through." The sympathy in her voice softened her intensity a few notches. "Zach wants all hands on deck to lock this jerk away for his lifetime."

Was that her explanation as to why she didn't want to tell Zach about the pregnancy yet? She didn't want to disappoint her boss?

"Hear me out on this, Jordan. Okay?" Her eyes pleaded.

He nodded.

"I'm serious. Don't give me that nod you do when you're only half listening," she warned.

His hands went up, palms out, in the surrender position.

"What if I don't work? What if I take leave? What if *I'm* the reason someone dies?" Her voice rose, along with her blood pressure, based on the heat crawling up her neck.

"What if something happens to you or the baby because of the case? Zach would never forgive himself." He may as well lay his cards on the table.

When she hesitated, he added, "This is Zach. You can ask him to keep the news under wraps. I'm not talking about taking an ad out in the paper or renting a billboard—"

"Yes, you are. No secret stays quiet for long in this town." She made a good point.

"There are a few people I trust. Zach is one of

them. He wouldn't even tell me if you asked him not to," he countered. "He wouldn't like being put in the position, but he would honor your wishes."

"I see your argument. Here's mine. I know my body, and I'm used to exercising. I have no problem consulting an OB about what's right and what's not right to do during the pregnancy. But if my doctor gives a thumbs-up to working and maintaining physical activity, you should know I plan to take that advice. As long as there's no risk to the child, I'll keep working at full capacity until it creates an unhealthy environment for the baby or I can't anymore." Her hands fisted, and he figured she probably didn't even realize it.

It was easy to see that she'd dug her heels in. There was no denying she'd thought this through the minute she realized it was a possibility, and he couldn't blame her when he really thought about her argument. If the shoe were on the other foot and a doctor told him it was safe to continue work on the ranch until the baby was born, he'd take the same stance.

An argument could be made that her work inherently put her in danger, but it was early in the pregnancy. He made a note to ask one of his sisters-in-law how she would deal with the situation. Jordan almost laughed out loud. His brother Deacon had married a strong-willed Fort Worth detective. Leah Cordon wouldn't back off her job unless she'd been forced. The same was true of Courtney.

"For now, promise me you won't tell Zach or anyone else about the pregnancy. I hear it's bad luck to talk about it before the second trimester anyway." Her eyes pleaded, and Jordan was reminded how easy it had been for her to get her way.

"And you'll make the announcement if the doctor says to?" He needed that much from her.

"I'd say happily, but I don't want to lie." Her shoulders slumped forward. "I just never thought this would happen to me."

"An unplanned pregnancy?" he asked.

"*Any* pregnancy. I was never that girl who dreamed about her wedding day or clipped out pictures of flowing white dresses," she admitted.

"You aren't exactly a tomboy, either." He wasn't sure why he felt the need to point it out.

"True. I liked some girly stuff. But parenthood? Jordan, come on. Are you seriously telling me you're ready for that commitment?" It was a fair question.

"What does the answer matter? It's here. This is what we have to deal with. It won't do any good to wish the situation would go away and that wouldn't be fair to the kid anyway." His honest answer seemed to deflate her shoulders a little more. A stab of guilt niggled at him. He could've put it more delicately. Damn, he could be a bull in a china shop without even trying.

"Promise me we won't be like my parents."

Those words struck like a physical blow.

COURTNEY WAITED FOR a response from Jordan. She studied his expression, and it was unreadable. "I should probably get back to work."

"I will love and care for any child that belongs to me but I'm more concerned about you right now. Promise me you'll take it easy?"

"I ride around in an SUV most of my shift. My other responsibility is talking to people. How bad can it get?" Coming back to her hometown had been meant to shield her from the harsher crimes in Dallas. But then no one knew for certain the Jacobstown Hacker had remained in town. He could've easily moved on. A little voice reminded her the odds of that happening were slim to none. That same voice insisted Jordan looked even better than she remembered, but that was probably heightened hormones and the fact that he was the father of her child. It was biology at work and nothing more.

Jordan stood, and she walked him to the door. He reached out and touched her arm as he stood a foot away from her. Suddenly, heat rushed through her body, and her skin sizzled with electric impulse. She instantly recoiled. If this was what she had to look forward to for the next seven or eight months, she was in for a real treat.

A few seconds of silence passed between them before Jordan spoke. "Be careful out there."

"Of course." She realized that her hand had come up to touch her belly when his gaze stopped there.

Jordan turned and walked out the door. It was like the moon covering the sun, eclipsing her in total darkness.

COURTNEY HAD HAD a day for the record books. First off, it was cold outside. She didn't *do* cold. This was Texas, land of eternal sunshine, and her blood was too thin for temperatures hovering above freezing.

Winds howled and tree branches snapped as pea-size hail dinged the hood of her SUV. It was getting late, but she didn't care. She exited the vehicle and turned on her flashlight. A hunch had led her to Rushing Creek. She'd received permission to be on the Kent property and had checked in with Isaac at the guard shack.

It was the kind of eerie night that felt like early fall, around Halloween. Clouds covered the moon, making it almost pitch-black outside.

A branch snapped behind her. Courtney spun around, weapon drawn and held along with her flashlight. What made the sound? An animal?

Courtney took a few steps toward the direction

of the sound. The trees were thick in this part of the land, making it a perfect place to hide. Was someone tracking her? The hairs on the back of her neck pricked.

A blast of frigid wind sent a shiver racing up her arms and down her back. Icy tendrils wrapped their long, lean fingers around her spine. Another crack sound sent her whirling to the left. Thoughts of a wild animal stalking her crossed her mind. Part of the reason she'd left Jacobstown was to get away from the country. It struck her as odd that this was the place she'd wanted to come back to.

Her cell buzzed. She didn't have a free hand, so she ignored it. Her radio was close to her ear and it had gone quiet. This was a good time to get the hell out of the woods. She'd call for backup if she could identify a threat. But then, she already knew the closest deputy was at least twenty minutes away. Courtney had grown up on the Kent property, having been friends with Amber and Amy in their teenage years.

What did it say that she hadn't contacted either one since returning home? Courtney tried to lie to herself and say it was because they were busy with lives of their own, but there was so much more to it. She'd gone behind everyone's backs when she had a fling with Jordan. It had been a wild seven days, and she'd gone out of her way since to avoid seeing her old friends. Besides, they'd barely kept up on social media. High school friends were just that. And Courtney didn't feel like she belonged in Jacobstown any more than she felt like she belonged in Dallas. It was strange to want to be part of something but always feel like the outsider looking in. Had it been that way her whole life?

Courtney backtracked, taking one step at a time and keeping watch where she'd heard the last branch snap. If wildlife was out there, and she knew it was, it wasn't getting her today. Slowly and cautiously, she eased one foot at a time. Her boots were heavy, but they kept her toes from freezing.

Wind whipped her hair, causing her ponytail to swish around and slap her in the face. She wished she'd pulled on a hat, because her ears felt like they were frostbitten already. It would also keep the ends of her hair out of her eyes.

This wasn't the time for a bout of nausea, but it happened anyway. Her stomach churned, and she thought about the fish tacos she'd eaten for dinner—she'd known even then that eating them could come back to haunt her. She'd chalked her craving up to stress but questioned the reason now. Was it the pregnancy?

And then she heard a voice. She froze, not wanting to draw attention to herself. She turned off her flashlight. Thoughts that never would have plagued her before the ambush in Dallas surfaced. An image of Breanna flashed in Courtney's mind, too.

Blood pumping, Courtney took another step backward. Her backside hit something hard. She sucked in a burst of air as she felt around, half expecting a blow to the head to follow. When none came and she felt the rough bark of a tree, she released the breath she'd been holding. She tried by sheer force of will to stop her hands from shaking.

Leaning against the tree in order to stay upright on rubbery legs, Courtney held back the urge to vomit. Bile rose in her throat, burning a hot trail as she palmed her service weapon. The Glock's metal was cold against her ungloved hand. She stood frozen, perfectly still for what felt like an eternity, waiting for the next sound.

A voice came over the radio, breaking the silence. The image of the young guy in Carolina-blue basketball shorts came to mind. As did the picture of Reggie Barstock shared by Zach McWilliams.

Another wave of nausea struck, harder this time. Courtney couldn't stop herself from folding forward and emptying the contents of her stomach. The taste of burning tacos lit her throat on fire. She had a feeling this would be the last time she could stomach tacos, which was unfortunate, because she loved them.

This time, when she came up for air, she saw someone dart behind a tree.

Chapter Five

"What are you doing on the south side of the property alone?" Jordan's warm voice cut through the cold air as he moved into view from behind the tree.

"My job," Courtney retorted, but she couldn't deny that she was relieved to see him. In fact, her nerves settled below panic. She'd never questioned her ability to handle any situation that came with being an officer of the law until recently, until the tragedy that had taken too many lives too early.

"Your job has you coming out here without backup?" It was a valid question. One she planned to dodge answering.

"Why are you here?" She stood straight and holstered her Glock. Then she tucked her flashlight into her belt.

He stood there staring her down for a minute, and she knew why. The question was whether or not he'd let her get away with a non-answer.

"Protecting my family's land," he finally said.

She leaned against the tree, and his expression took a dive.

"You okay?" He was at her side in a heartbeat. "You're freezing out here. Come back to the main house with me."

There was no use fighting it. She didn't want to be left alone, even though she'd eventually find her way back. She'd gotten herself turned around on the massive property. She'd been overconfident, and it had nearly cost her. She resolved not to make that mistake again.

"I'd like that," she admitted. "I just need a minute."

"Or I can give you a hand. My ATV isn't far from here." He froze. "Is it safe for you to ride one?"

"Should be fine," she reassured, and it warmed her heart more than she wanted to admit that he was concerned for her well-being.

Courtney let Jordan help her to the ATV.

"Take my gloves. Your hands are like icicles," he said.

She'd argue, but he was right. "What will you use?"

"I'll be fine until I get home. How long have you been out here?" He took off his gloves and handed the pair to her.

"An hour. Maybe more." She took the offerings and felt an immediate difference as soon as she slid them on her fingers. They were already warm from his hands, and it instantly felt like someone held her hands over a campfire. "Ah, thank you for these. I didn't realize a pair of gloves could feel so wonderful."

An emotion flickered behind his eyes that she couldn't quite pinpoint. His tough facade returned almost immediately as he said, "Hop on the back. It'll take about thirty minutes to reach home, so get comfortable."

Courtney did as he said and scooted back far enough for him to throw his leg over and take the driver's position. He was true to his word. They arrived at the main house almost a half hour on the dot later. She briefly prayed no one else was home, but the thought of being alone with Jordan again didn't sit well, either. On balance, she figured it was best if they had company. From the last time she was there, she remembered Kents coming and going almost constantly. Good. She didn't trust herself not to say the wrong thing while the two of them were getting their footing in this new... *reality*, for lack of a better word.

The main house had a fire going in the fireplace in the kitchen. Courtney made her way to it quickly, taking off Jordan's gloves and placing them on the hearth next to her.

"Can I take your coat?" Jordan stood close enough for her to feel a different kind of heat.

She shrugged out of her jacket and handed it over to him.

"How about something warm to drink?" he asked.

"Any chance your sister keeps any chamomile in the pantry?" She rubbed her hands together in front of the flame.

"I wouldn't know. I can check." His intense eyes had a way of looking right through her, so she sidestepped his gaze and moved back to the fireplace, where she kept her back to him. She removed her belt and felt instant relief from not having to carry the extra weight around. Her shoulder holster came off next. She placed those items on a dining chair before she reclaimed her seat on the hearth. The warmth from the fire started immediately thawing out her frozen limbs. She flexed and released her hands, trying to expedite the return of feeling to her fingers.

Jordan went to work pouring himself a cup of coffee—the smell of which didn't do great things to her stomach—while a pot of water came to boil on the stove. "I don't know what to do besides pour the water into a cup over the tea bag."

"It's pretty much that simple." The smell of supper still lingered in the kitchen, and her stomach growled.

"Are you hungry?" he asked.

She'd be embarrassed by the fact her stomach

had just announced that it was empty, but that ship had probably sailed, considering it hadn't been all that long ago that the two of them lay naked and tangled in the sheets of her uncle's fishing cabin. She could lie about the fact that she could eat an entire side of beef courtesy of pregnancy hormones or come clean and admit to being hungry again. At least she hoped this weird vomit-eat-nausea-eat-vomit-eat routine could be attributed to something that made sense. "Soup sounds good. And a toothbrush if you have a spare."

"You remember where that is?" It was more statement than question.

There were always extras in the guest bathroom. The Kent family was prepared for just about anything. Once, when the town lost power due to flooding after one of the wettest springs on record, the Kent family hosted a barbecue to feed as many folks as possible. Their generator allowed them to open their home to the elderly and mothers with small children until the power company could sort out the issue and restore electricity. The Kents had always been good people, and she was sorry to hear they'd passed away. She couldn't imagine seeing one without the other.

"Yes, down the hall." She mentally nudged herself out of the reverie. "I'll be right back."

The toothbrush and toothpaste felt like gifts from heaven as she splashed cold water on her face, rinsed her mouth and then brushed. Being here in the main house with Jordan after their fling and recent news should feel stranger than it did. She chalked it up to having been there before in her teenage years and tried to forget it. She sent an update to Zach via text, noting that she'd found nothing by the creek.

By the time she returned to the kitchen, there was a cup of tea sitting on the table. She took a seat near the fireplace and stared at the folded stack of clothes she recognized as belonging to her.

"You left those at the cabin. I had them cleaned." There was an edge to his voice that she recognized from their earlier conversation. Nothing about this day was going right. Sure, he'd been on her mind. And now it seemed everywhere she turned, he wasn't far. To be fair, she was on his ranch. It wasn't like he was stalking her.

Of course, she was grateful for bumping into him on the property tonight. For the first time in her career when she'd come upon a possibly sketchy situation, she'd frozen.

After her friends had been ambushed in the protest that had turned deadly last year, nothing was the same. She couldn't rely on her body to cooperate when her stress levels skyrocketed.

"Thanks, but I should probably—"

"Hear me out before you finish." He put up a hand in protest.

She picked up her cup of tea and took a sip, already feeling more relaxed than she'd felt in longer than she could remember. Well, that wasn't entirely true, because she'd felt pretty darn comfortable in his arms during their fling. Jordan had a way of putting her at ease, and she knew better than to get comfortable in the feeling. She nodded, hoping her cheeks weren't flushing thinking about the amazing sex they'd had for seven days and nights that had gone by way too fast.

"We have everything you could possibly want or need right here." He didn't mention that he could keep an eye on her, but she figured that had to be part of the motivation.

"I have a home to go to, Jordan. What about that?"

"You don't have any pets to take care of, so you could always go home tomorrow morning." He made a good point.

"Why should I stay here? I have a perfectly good bed—"

"Because I'm asking you to." He held out his hands, palms up. "I'll admit that I got hit with what felt like a boulder earlier, and I doubt that I reacted the best way I could've. I'm sorry for that."

"There's no right way to find out you're going to be a dad unexpectedly," she offered. He was beating himself up for nothing. The news had caught them both off guard, and she hadn't exactly been dealing with it well, either.

"And then there's the murder investigation…"

"Breanna." It was difficult to say her name without getting choked up.

"Right. I know it's your job to investigate, and I respect that. But you'll go home to an empty house, and you shouldn't be alone right now. This news hit you, too. I remember what you said about not ever wanting to be a mother." The rim of his coffee cup suddenly became very interesting.

"You feel responsible for this?" Of course he did. Guilt was written across the worry lines on his forehead. "Wait. Don't answer that question. It's obvious that you do, so I just want to remind you that it takes two people to make a baby."

"That part I'm aware of." He smirked, and it was devastatingly handsome. She didn't want it to tug at her heart, but it did. "Like it or not, we're in this together."

"What's that supposed to mean?" she asked.

"I remember what happened when you tried to sleep—"

"People have bad dreams," she said, a little too quickly. She could feel tension in her shoulder blades, especially on the left side, which sent pain up her neck and threatened to give her a terrible stress headache.

"That's not how I'd describe what I saw you

experience." Great, now he was an armchair psychologist?

"I'm okay." Her body belied her words, trembling just thinking about the nightmares.

JORDAN COULD SEE Courtney's body shaking. Hell, he wasn't trying to upset her. "I'm probably going about this all wrong. But I'd like you to stay the night so I can make sure you're okay. You're in the middle of a tough investigation, and you got hit with news I know you weren't expecting or wanting. You just started your job here at Zach's office, and now you're going to have to take time off at some point for maternity leave. It's more than most could handle, but this is you, Courtney. You're one of the strongest women I know—"

Courtney's face was turning redder and redder with every word he spoke. He seemed to be making a mess of things.

"I'm not here to make things worse. At least let me feed you before you run out of here," he said by way of compromise.

She nodded, and he wouldn't look a gift horse in the mouth. He finished heating dinner and set a bowl of soup on the table for her. She finished it within minutes.

"Thank you. It was amazing," she said. "I can't remember the last time I was this tired. I'll take you up on the offer to stay the night if it still stands. I'm too tired to get behind the wheel, and it has been a long day. Taking a shower and then dropping into bed sounds like heaven about now."

"You already know where the guest room is. Clothes are there." He motioned toward the stack. "You need anything else, just give a shout. Someone is always around."

"Will do. Can I help clean up in here first?" she asked.

"I got this." He shook his head for emphasis.

She picked up the folded stack and disappeared down the hallway. The freshly-made soup provided the first smile since Courtney arrived at KR. His chest puffed out with pride for giving her something to make her feel better.

Co-parenting would require that the parents actually get along. Making progress on their complicated relationship felt good. Jordan had had the benefit of growing up with parents who'd loved each other. Although their life together as a couple hadn't always been easy, his parents cared for their family and the community. Their reputation for generosity was one Jordan and his siblings intended to uphold. Being a Kent meant walking in big shoes, but Jordan had every intention of living up to his family name.

Of course, he wasn't exactly doing a stellar job of it so far. The pregnancy news had caught him off guard, tipped his world off its axis. Getting married because of a child was noble but not exactly the recipe for a happy relationship. He couldn't even imagine growing up in a household where the parents weren't head-over-heels in love with each other. Besides, Courtney seemed more opposed to the idea of marriage for a child's sake than he did.

Jordan had some work to do in order to gain Courtney's trust. But then, she didn't seem capable of trusting anyone after her upbringing and then what had happened in Dallas. He'd learned about what had happened to her and then read the story in the news following their brief fling. She'd been the lone survivor of a terrible tragedy, the kind of heartbreak that changed a person's view on life. The fact that she'd survived when several of her team didn't seemed to weigh heavy on her. He could imagine that came with the kind of guilt that could swallow a person whole.

Jordan finished with the dishes and drained his coffee mug. His thoughts bounced from Breanna and her family and back to Courtney. There was no way he'd get any shut-eye with all that was rattling around in his mind. Shutting down his brain would be next to impossible. He took a shower to help clear his thoughts and then changed into clean clothes.

There was no use fighting his urge to stay awake. He'd learned a long time ago that it was easier to go with the flow. So he settled down at the kitchen table with his laptop and a notebook. He tried to think back to who Breanna's friends had been. He was drawing a blank. For as long as he could remember, she'd been a loner. And then there was Reggie Barstock. He had a limp on his left side, a grudge, and seemed to slip in and out of town without being seen. Jordan's sister-in-law Chelsea was a distant relative and had inherited the Barstock family home and business. Trouble from Reggie had followed, but then Chelsea's ex-husband had come to town and tried to scare her into getting back together with him.

It was that incident that had brought Chelsea and Jordan's brother Nate together. Nate was a volunteer firefighter. The two had met and then fallen in love after Nate answered a call from dispatch not long after Chelsea moved to the area. Her craft pizza place had opened downtown last year after a fire nearly took her life. Everyone had suspected Reggie Barstock, but he'd been innocent. Her ex, Travis, had been responsible.

Barstock could stay on the suspect list. Courtney had mentioned someone who lived on the edge of town, a former truck driver. Jordan made a note to ask Zach about the guy.

Didn't Courtney mention something about following someone in blue shorts at The Mart? He'd ask her about that later. Although she might not speak to someone outside of law enforcement on an ongoing investigation. The fact that a murder had happened on Kent land made this personal. He figured he'd stick around this time in order to pitch in to find the murderer. He recapped the situation in his mind. A guy started out by killing small animals before moving onto larger ones, the heifers. And then he killed a woman.

Jordan wrote down, *has a problem with women*. He leaned over and picked up his laptop. He opened it and powered it up. Then, he looked up "characteristics of serial killers" before skimming the results. Working for the family ranch at the Idaho location gave him flexibility with his job.

Based on the search, he scribbled down a few key words and phrases that caught his attention. *Easily bored. Lacks empathy. Remorseless. Superficially charming. Grandiose. There weren't many but they impacted society most.*

Questions swirled, so he wrote those down, too. Could the person everyone was looking for be someone young? Someone in his early twenties? Or maybe someone who went away to school but came home for breaks? What was the tie to Jacobstown? Why did he cut off the left foot? Was he born deformed? Ridiculed? Was he injured at a young age? Teased?

There was no doubt these same questions had been asked by his cousin Zach. There was also no doubt that Zach was working toward answers. More questions struck, so he jotted those down, too. What was the killer's next move? Was this guy looking for some kind of a prize?

Damn. That one hit hard and fast. Since the killing happened on Kent property, Jordan had to assume the guy was somehow connected to the land or the family. The jerk was butchering livestock and then a woman under their noses. He couldn't even think about Breanna's murder without being slammed with anger. Even with increased security and strategically placed cameras, the guy had gotten away with murder.

Of course, the Kent ranch was sprawled out over thousands of acres and spread into three states: Texas, Idaho and Wyoming. As far as anyone knew, this guy had only struck in Texas. He'd hit other ranches in the area. So he must be tied to the community in Jacobstown. He also seemed to have an affinity for water, specifically the creek. Jordan jotted that down, too. It seemed a case like this could use as many eyes on it as possible.

He made a note to talk to every woman in the Kent family. It wasn't safe for any one of them to be out alone until this jerk was safely behind bars. A Kent would be considered a prize due to the family's status in the community. There was no way Jordan was willing to wait for something to happen to someone he loved in order to find out.

A question burned. Why start killing now? Didn't serial killers always have some kind of trigger? The event that sent this man spiraling might've happened on that date.

But then, the holidays played a number on a lot of people's emotions. It might be that simple. The date had more to do with leading up to Christmas.

These were all easy questions to ask and assumptions to make. Jordan was certain his cousin would've thought of everything written in the notebook. Maybe this case required more out-of-the-box thinking. Dates could represent an anniversary or could be some kind of twisted code. Then again, people got depressed around the holidays. Jordan had read somewhere that depression spiked this time of year. Which also made him think this could be the anniversary of the death of something.

The method of also killing had to have some type of meaning attached to it. The killer had used a weapon with a sharp, clean edge. A hatchet?

With half the town pitching in to take shifts on neighborhood watch groups or volunteer at Zach's office, there were more folks outside than usual. Zach had also said a few folks were getting out of Jacobstown for a while, saying they felt safer going to Colorado or New Mexico to ski rather than stick around town this year.

Jordan glanced at the time. It was half past two in the morning. Zach would most likely be sleeping, so disturbing him in order to discuss the case was out of the question. Courtney was in the guest room, hopefully asleep. It was most likely the pregnancy, but he'd never seen her look so tired. His heart stirred thinking about her, but he shut it down quickly. It wouldn't do any good re-membering how soft her creamy skin was when she settled in the crook of his arm to sleep. Or how much he actually liked staying awake into ridicu-lous hours of the morning talking. Or how fiery hot the sex had been.

A cold glass of milk later, and he settled down at the table again.

A pad of paper stared back at him.

A bloodcurdling scream got him to his feet and moving down the hall faster than a thoroughbred at Lone Star Park.

Chapter Six

Courtney sat up and pulled the covers up to her neck. She felt disoriented and like her head might split in two. She tried to stop her body from shaking as the bedroom door burst open. A familiar face—Jordan's—was next to her bed barely a second later.

"Are you okay?" he asked.

"I'm good." But she was not all right. And part of her feared she never would be again. Beads of sweat trickled down her forehead, and she realized that she must've screamed for him to come running in like he did.

More sweat beaded, rolling down the side of her face, and she could feel that she'd soaked her shirt.

Slowly, her bearings started to come back. She was at Jordan Kent's family home. It was the middle of the night. She was sleeping in his guest room. The night terrors that had plagued her for the past year were relentless.

"You're safe now." Jordan said other words meant to soothe her as the mattress dipped under his weight. He sat next to her, and she instantly felt the air charge around her. Attraction replaced fear. She didn't debate her next actions. His arms opened to her, and she embraced the invitation, burying her face in his masculine chest.

Memories flooded her as she breathed in his all-male, uniquely Jordan scent. It was a mix of coffee and campfires, outdoorsy and spicy. She missed that smell. It would be so easy to get lost in it now and let Jordan be her strength. She was tired. Tired of being the strong one. Tired of standing alone. Tired of missing him.

There was a baby to think about now. A child who would have a better life than Courtney had had. She took in a breath meant to fortify her but only ushered in more of Jordan's scent. That was about as productive as trying to milk a beetle.

Pulling on all the strength she had left, she moved away from him and hugged her knees to her chest. "I'm sorry about that. I won't make it a habit."

"Promise me that anytime you need someone to lean on, you'll call me." There was so much honesty and purity in the words, she almost gave in. But that would mean so much more than the surface of being there for a friend. Trusting *anyone* wasn't her gig. Some people weren't made like that, and she was one of them. Growing up with an abusive father after her mother had abandoned her wasn't an excuse, but she figured it didn't help.

Those weren't the words he needed to hear based on his frown, and yet she couldn't lie to him, either. Instead of agreeing, she took a breath. "They're getting better. The nightmares. They're not as vivid anymore."

"That's good." The edge returned to his voice, and she wondered if he felt the sting of rejection. She didn't mean it that way, but if the shoe were on the other foot, she'd probably take it the same.

"It's just something I have to handle. You know?" She hoped he could understand, because she really wasn't trying to be a jerk. Letting anyone else in was just hard…too hard.

He nodded by way of response, and she appreciated the fact that he was making the effort.

It didn't help that Jordan Kent had a reputation for sticking around for no one without the last name of Kent or McWilliams. He'd never been the relationship type—not that he was offering anything permanent to her. Granted, he'd made it clear that he'd be there for his child. She'd never doubted him for a second on that front. And there were so many other reasons rolling around inside her head that made her fear they would end up disliking each other if she stuck around long enough. For one, the two of them were from different worlds, different sides of the track and different backgrounds. Those differences were bound to cause arguments and drive a wedge between them. It was only a matter of time before he realized it, too.

But this wasn't the right time to bring any of that up.

"I think it's the case dredging up stress. That and the pregnancy," she admitted.

He nodded and stared intently at a patch of wall across the room.

"Thanks for coming in and checking on me," she said, trying to soften her reaction.

He must've taken it as a dismissal, because he pushed off the bed and crossed the room. She was speechless as she watched him prepare to walk out. She struggled to string together a sentence. Her heart pounded against her ribs, and all her warning flares fired at the same time. "Stay with me. Please. I don't really want to be alone right now."

"Have you spoken to anyone about the night terrors?" He stopped but didn't turn around.

"No. But I planned to," she said a little too quickly. It sounded desperate even to her. "I know what you said before in the cabin, and I heard you—"

"Save it." The disappointment in his voice was a knife to the chest.

She expected him to walk right out the door. Instead, he turned around and came back to bed. He sat on the edge with his back to her, silent.

A torrent of words came to mind, but Courtney

knew better than to open the floodgates. So she sat there, too. Quiet. Waiting. Hoping?

A minute passed, maybe two. Courtney shut her eyes and massaged her temples, but her hands were still shaking too badly to manage it for long. She brought her hands down to her lap.

Jordan eased beside her and stretched out his long legs. He had on jeans and no shirt, like she'd seen him do the week in the cabin. Her body trembled, and the quake started slowly.

"Courtney, are you okay?" There was concern in his voice—a voice that was bringing her back from the brink. Fall into the abyss and she'd be no use to anyone for days. The darkness threatened to suck her under, and her insides felt like she was paddling madly to keep her head above water. It also felt like there was an anchor tied around her ankle that was tugging her toward the ocean floor.

"Yes," she managed to get out on a burst of air. She flexed and released her fingers, needing to feel something besides the sensation of drowning. Panic was building from deep in her bones. Her muscles tensed, and there was a kink in her left shoulder that no amount of yoga stretching could ease.

"Hey, you don't sound…" His lips were still moving, but a ringing noise in her ears drowned out everything else in the room.

At this point, thinking would do her no good. She needed something to ground her, to root her back in reality and crack the concrete hardening around her brain causing her to go into fight, flight or freeze mode without being provoked. There was something stirring in the pit of her stomach. Her nervous system was on autopilot, which also meant heightened alert.

She blinked, trying to slow the kaleidoscope of images—images that had haunted her for the past year like a stalker in a dark alley. The world felt like it had tipped on its axis, spinning out of control. Instinct had her trying to grab hold of something, *anything* to keep her grounded.

Without thinking, she climbed onto Jordan's lap and kissed him. She pressed her lips to his and tunneled her fingers into his dark, curly mane. At first, his body tensed, but it didn't take much cajoling to get him to kiss her back. She parted her lips for him, and he slid his tongue in her mouth. He tasted like peppermint toothpaste and coffee, her favorite two things combined. A wall of memories crashed down around her with his clean, masculine scent filling her senses every time she took a breath.

An ache from deep within sprang up, catching her off guard. She'd missed the sex, and part of her could admit to how badly she'd missed Jordan, even though she tried to convince herself that she'd confused him with the feeling of home. *He* represented home to her. But the side to her that didn't accept nonsense called her out on it. She missed

Jordan. She missed the feel of his arms around her. She missed the way he tasted, and she missed their conversations that ran too late into the night. Seeing the sunrise and laughing about being up all night had never held so much appeal as when she'd been with him.

For a little while, her demons receded, and she felt normal again. The nightmares didn't stop completely, but they were better that week. He tried to get her to talk about them, and she'd gotten so used to dodging the subject. When she saw the hurt in his eyes, she put up the walls.

Jordan's hands looped around her waist as the kiss intensified. All other thoughts drifted into background noise in her head. Everything calmed, and she was consumed by the need to kiss him harder.

And then he picked her up and sat her next to him.

JORDAN HAD ALMOST taken another trip down the rabbit hole with Courtney. He wasn't sure when he'd developed this strong of a conscience when it came to turning down mind-blowing consensual sex, but somewhere along the line he'd picked one up. Damned if he knew where or why. The timing couldn't have been worse, because Courtney was smart, beautiful and beyond sexy.

Both of them sat on the bed, breathing hot and heavy. He cursed himself more than once for slowing down that runaway train, but he knew that sex would only confuse the issues between them. And his bruised ego wanted her to want *him* and not just another round of casual sex.

As he sat there next to one of the most beautiful women he knew, he realized he'd be cursing that niggle of conscience for days. There it was. He'd stopped something from happening that he'd wanted ever since he left the cabin. He couldn't take his actions back now, either.

So he apologized instead.

"Why are you sorry?" She sounded offended.

"I don't want to take advantage of you while you're vulnerable," he said.

"Pregnancy hasn't made me weak—"

"I wasn't talking about that. You had one of your nightmares." She'd refused to talk about them before, and he figured this time would be no different.

He glanced over in time to see her staring at the wall. She repositioned to where her back was against the headboard again and pulled the covers up. "They started after..."

Jordan took her hand in his. Hers was shaking.

"What happened in Dallas shook me up. I lost friends who were like family that day." This was the most she'd said so far. She'd refused to talk about the incident while at the cabin.

"That would be hard for anyone." She was strong and needed to hear confirmation.

"The department offered counseling." She blew

out a breath. "*Offered* is putting it lightly. My job depended on me attending sessions."

"Did it help?" he asked.

"I said what I had to in order to get my file rubber-stamped so I could get back to work." She pulled her hand away. "I lied and said I was okay. That I'd had a few bad dreams but was getting better."

"The counselor believed you?"

"My job depended on it." She shrugged. "I was pretty convincing. Cops always joke about what we'd say if the time came, so I had a few lines rehearsed. I did a little research, and it wasn't hard to figure out what he wanted to hear. I mean, how stupid does the department think a cop is? Say the wrong thing and bye-bye pension. Everything in the session goes into our permanent work file. No one who needs a job is going to be completely honest in a situation like that. We can't afford to be. It could ruin our careers."

He understood the logic and figured it was pretty common among law enforcement officers and military personnel. The upside to this conversation was that she was opening up to him a little. This was a start toward building a bridge of trust between the two of them. Jordan would take any progress he could get. Walking away from his child would never be a consideration. He needed to forge a relationship with Courtney for the sake of their child.

"How about private counseling?" He knew he'd made a mistake in asking the second she recoiled.

"Thanks for checking on me, Jordan. I had a moment, but I promise I'm feeling better now." Her tone left no room for doubt that she'd put up the walls between them again.

He needed to choose his next words carefully. "Believe it or not, I wasn't trying to insult you by asking the question—"

"I never said you were." She stretched and yawned, and he could tell it was fake.

"Courtney," he started, but the right words didn't come. The last thing he wanted was to make the situation worse.

She rolled onto her side, facing away from him.

His bruised ego told him to get up and walk out the door. But she hadn't asked him to leave, so he wondered if she was pushing him away because she didn't want him around or if she was too scared to talk about what had happened that sent her into this tailspin.

So he laid down beside her and pulled her against him. Her muscles stiffened just enough for him to tell before he could feel her exhale and relax against him. Neither spoke, and that was okay with him.

It didn't take long for her slow, steady breathing to tell him that she'd drifted off to sleep again. He shouldn't breathe in the floral scent of her thick red hair. He shouldn't let that fill his senses.

She was unavailable. He realized that was probably half of the attraction he'd felt toward her early on. He'd never been one to want to stick around the morning after a round of hot sex. He certainly hadn't been looking for anything more than a few days of the best sex of his life.

There'd been something broken in her that had connected with the broken parts of him. Their connection had gone beyond physical.

But then, he didn't make a habit of bedding friends from the past. Jordan was all about moving forward, grabbing on to the next goal without time to think about settling in or settling down. And that hadn't changed just because he'd wanted more than a string of hot nights with Courtney. If anything, he realized just how fine he'd been without being tied down in a relationship when he'd gone back to Idaho and to his work on the family ranch there.

Jordan woke with the sun shining brightly through the window. He didn't realize that he'd dozed off. He'd gotten too comfortable. All he felt was Courtney's warm body flush with his. His heart stirred—and that wasn't the only thing awake and reminding him he was alive and well.

He gently peeled her off him and slid out of the covers as quietly as he could manage. Her steady breathing said she was still asleep. He couldn't help but notice how peaceful she looked lying there. It

pained him to get out of bed, but he wanted to discuss the case with Zach before she woke.

Besides, he reminded himself not to get too
cozy with Courtney. His heart couldn't take getting attached and watching her walk away a second time.

Damn. Where'd that come from?

Jordan freshened up, brushed his teeth and then
moved into the kitchen. He located his cell, filled
his mug with a fresh cup of coffee and then called
Zach.

"Morning," Zach answered. His cousin sounded
like he was running on a couple hours of sleep. The
mounting pressure from the anniversary of Breanna's death that loomed was evident in his tone.

"I know you're busy, so I'll get right to the reason I called," Jordan said after returning the greeting.

"What's up?" Zach asked.

"I've been getting up to speed on the Jacobstown Hacker case. I'd like to pitch in to help in any
way I can. I'm home now, and plan to stick around
for a while." Jordan paused a beat.

"Welcome home, cousin." Zach and Jordan had
been close growing up, and his cousin had asked
more than once why Jordan didn't come back to
Jacobstown to live.

The town didn't feel like home, even though this

was where he'd been born and bred. "What can I do to help with the investigation?"

"We need as many eyes on as much of Rushing Creek as we can muster," Zach stated. "No lone wolves, though. I want everyone to buddy up. It's even better if people go out in teams and take a coordinated approach. If you see or hear anything suspicious, be smart about investigating. We're making the assumption that the suspect is armed and dangerous. Call me immediately if you think you've come across him, no matter where you are and no matter what time of day or night."

"You can count on it. But it seems less likely that he'd return to Rushing Creek with all the attention he has to know will be there," Jordan surmised.

"True," Zach agreed. "Our community presence can deter crime. This guy is opportunistic. The fewer options he has, the better, which is also a reason we're encouraging everyone to go out in groups as much as possible."

"Makes sense. Did he kill Breanna prior to bringing her to the scene on the ranch?" Jordan's suspicions about the kind of person they were dealing with were being confirmed.

"There's no sign of blood leading up to or away from the crime scene. If he killed Breanna and waited until he was at the creek to use the cutting instrument on her ankle, there wouldn't be a trail."

"All we know about the man so far is that he's moved on to human targets. We also know his left leg or foot is significant," Zach informed.

"How did you figure that out?" Jordan knew his cousin had already checked out obvious suspects and would've sifted through as much evidence as he could find.

"Impressions in the dirt. He puts more weight on his right side, based on the data Deputy Lopez collected. He was able to measure the impressions in the soil from his footprints and noticed a difference in depth." There was no doubt Zach was one of the best at his job. What if the killer knew Zach? The man could be a volunteer. Jordan had read that killers often volunteered to help in searches when victims went missing. It was a way of keeping tabs on the investigation while being arrogant. Those killers seemed to get a thrill out of being right under law enforcement's nose.

"Which has to be a large part of the reason everyone keeps circling back to Reggie Barstock. We already know he has an issue with his left foot." Jordan paused as Zach confirmed. "Is anyone aware of Barstock's current location?"

"His whereabouts are unknown, but I've been getting reports from folks who think they see him every few days and it turns out to be nothing. Courtney reported seeing a younger man with a limp in Bexford. We've been watching for his vehicle but haven't had any hits there," Zach supplied. "I asked Liesel to notify me if Reggie shows up at the diner, where I last saw him. My deputies have been spreading the word if a barista, gas station attendant or waitress sees Barstock to notify me immediately."

"What if it's not Barstock?" The idea had to be considered.

"That's the problem. If everyone's looking for a red shoe, the green one slips under the radar." Zach had just voiced Jordan's concern. "Gus Stanton is a person of interest—"

"He's the former truck driver," Jordan said.

"That's right. You must've heard about him." Zach didn't sound surprised, which made Jordan wonder if his cousin knew about the relationship with Courtney.

"He came to mind. I actually ran into Courtney the other day in Bexford," Jordan informed.

Zach perked up. "If he makes the trip once a week like most people, the next time he's at the store, the anniversary will have passed." Zach's voice sounded like a headache was working up. "Do you have a description of this guy?"

"That I don't. Courtney said it was probably nothing, but I figure it can't hurt to talk about." He was tossing every idea out in hopes something would stick.

"She was in a bad state yesterday. The food poisoning seemed to have hit her hard. When you saw her, did she look like she was doing any better?"

"Nothing worse than getting a hold of a bad batch of food. Stomach pain is the worst." Jordan dodged the question. Guilt hit him harder than if he'd been on a motorcycle going a hundred miles an hour and slammed into a brick wall. Going along with her food poisoning story made him feel like a jerk. Jordan needed to get the conversation back on track and away from the landmine that had anything to do with his knowledge of or relationship with Courtney. "What else should I be on the lookout for? Is there a profile on this guy?"

"The only thing I know for certain is that he'll kill again…" Zach's voice trailed off at the end.

"There any chance he's already behind bars for another crime?" Jordan offered.

"It's possible but highly unlikely with this guy's skills," Zach said.

"What if he's done? What if he built up to killing a person, did it and then decided it was too much or that he'd gone too far?" Jordan tossed a few more ideas out there.

"My fear is that he's only just whetted his appetite. I believe Breanna was his first murder, and he's gotten a taste of what it's like. He might even realize what he did was wrong. But he won't stop, because he *can't*. There's no question in my mind that he fits the profile of a serial killer. There's typically a cooling-off period in between murders, but he seems to be working faster. In this case, we don't have a lot to go on. We don't know enough to get a clear picture of the guy. You already know about as much as we do. Other than the fact that he fits the personality type to a T, I don't have much else to tell you." There was so much frustration in his voice. Zach was a great sheriff and an even better person. It was easy to realize that he'd take this personally.

"We'll get this jerk before he hurts someone else." It was a promise Jordan meant but had no idea if he could keep.

"I hope so."

"Before we hang up, I have to ask." Jordan paused for acknowledgment. Continued after it came, "How safe are the Kent women?"

"You read my mind if you're thinking one of them could be his next target." Zach issued a sharp sigh. "In fact, now that you mention it, we should have every one of them send in a list of anyone they know who might have a beef with them from the past. This goes way back."

"I'll send out a text. I was also thinking we should make sure each Kent woman is protected," Jordan added.

"The best way to ensure safety is the buddy system. No one should be outside alone, and that even means when on the property," Zach said.

"Especially when on the ranch," Jordan concurred.

"Hell, until this jerk is caught, I don't want anyone in this county going outside alone. I think every man and woman needs to be accounted for at all times..." Zach's voice trailed off. His fear was evident in his tone. All signs pointed to the killer targeting another woman, but he could change tracks to mix things up. It was highly unlikely but everyone needed to take precautions. Jordan heard his cousin's cell make a noise. "Hold on, I'm getting a text from Ellen."

Jordan sent off a text to his family making the request for all Kents to use extra caution and stick with a group at all times. He made a special note the victim was a woman, as were the heifers. If this guy was looking for a prize, he was going to have to look further than the Kents.

Zach returned to the line. "I was hoping to avoid a widespread panic in town. It seems it's too late for that."

"What happened?" Jordan figured every woman in the county was concerned about safety.

"I've had four missing-person reports in the last twenty minutes from concerned parents and husbands. *Four.* All of whom were found either in the yard, in another part of the house or checking the mailbox when Ellen asked them to look." Zach's voice was weary.

"The next few days are going to be a challenge until this jerk is locked behind bars," Jordan agreed. He was probably being optimistic about the timing.

"Let's just keep everyone alive and calm." Zach rarely admitted defeat, but it was obvious this case was wearing on him. "It just occurred to me that I need to have my deputies double up as much as possible"

"If you're worried about Courtney, she's tough, and she carries a weapon. She has training to back it up. This guy doesn't seem to like a fighter," Jordan said. Courtney being put on desk duty would ease Jordan's stress, but he highly doubted she would stand for it while a dangerous criminal stalked the town.

"Those are excellent points, but I take the safety of all my deputies very seriously, man or woman. I don't want her to worry that I think she's not capable of doing her job, but she worries be because she's still figuring out the lay of the land around here. Being away from town for so many years and new to the department puts her at a disadvantage. I'll have to give this situation a little more thought before I make a decision."

Jordan figured his cousin would have even more concern about her if he knew Courtney was pregnant. For one tempting moment, he thought about sharing the news. But going behind her back wouldn't create the kind of trust they needed to bring up a child together. And Jordan would never betray his word. "We'll pull together like we always do. This town is strong, and the people here are some of the best humans I know. The panic is understandable, but it will subside. In the meantime, we'll catch this jerk and lock him away where he can't hurt anyone else."

"I appreciate your willingness to pitch in and help, Jordan. I really do. I know this time of year is busy on the ranch and hard on everyone in the family. I miss my aunt and uncle more than I can put into words," he said.

"We got past another Christmas and into a New Year." Jordan felt a gut punch just thinking about how much he missed his parents. Time was supposed to make this easier. In this case, it didn't. He missed his family even more, and it probably had to do with the fact that his siblings had all moved on and started families of their own. He'd been the odd man out for most of his life, and that was certainly true again.

As he said goodbye and ended the call, he glanced up in time to see Courtney emerge from the hallway.

Seeing her standing there in her T-shirt and boxers stirred him in dangerous places—places better left for dead.

Chapter Seven

Courtney stared at Jordan. His bottom lip had jutted out for a quick second, which meant he didn't want to tell her something.

"What is it?" she demanded.

"That was Zach—"

"You didn't tell him anything about us, did you?" Dread was a heavy blanket around her shoulders, and panic was a galloping horse in her chest.

"Of course not. But that doesn't mean I like keeping secrets while talking to my family." He turned away from her. The look on his face, the honest pain in that one sentence, struck her like a physical blow. Was she being selfish?

"I'm sorry for putting you in that position, Jordan. I really am." Although she knew that announcing a pregnancy before the second trimester was considered bad luck, it was odd to be focused on superstition when she didn't want to be in this condition in the first place. She glanced down at her stomach and realized that she was touching her belly.

Did part of her—a part tucked deep down inside—secretly wish for a family? A *real* family and not two people who couldn't get along, not a mother who cowered and took unimaginable abuse from her husband?

Jordan was right to stop things before they got out of hand last night after that kiss. She needed to remember there was more at stake than an embarrassing morning after if they gave in to passion again. And she wouldn't risk her child's emotional stability to satisfy her own desire, no matter how strong her want for Jordan Kent was.

Jordan pushed back from the kitchen table and stood. "Are you hungry? I could fry up a couple of eggs."

"My stomach is still a little queasy. Do you have any yogurt?" That much she could keep down.

"In the fridge." He motioned toward it, so she helped herself. "Zach and I talked about the fact that this creep seems focused on women. With the crimes happening on or near Rushing Creek, we're concerned about him wanting a prize. All women and especially a Kent should take extra precautions until he's behind bars."

"That's good advice. Did he mention anything

else?" She took another bite of the creamy vanilla blend.

"His phone at the office is starting to blow up. If someone's wife or daughter is in the next room and doesn't answer the first time a person calls out, his office is getting a panicked phone call." Jordan knew how much that would take away from manpower that could be focused on something more important. Trained volunteers were a good thing to have, and he hoped they'd help more than get in the way.

"Maybe I should go in to work today," she said.

"It's your day off. Besides, you won't do anyone good if you're sick," he quickly countered. He was right. She knew it. But she wished it wasn't true. Sitting on the sidelines was driving her a little crazy.

"The yogurt is helping." That part was true. She felt useless, and keeping busy was the best way to keep the darkness at bay. She crossed and then uncrossed her legs before tapping her finger on the table.

Bemused, Jordan stared at her.

"What?" She asked but she wasn't sure she wanted to know the answer to the question.

"You're not used to taking a lazy day, are you?" He was spot-on.

"Nope. I tend to pace or clean out a closet or something exciting like that."

"That why your house was spotless?" He walked to the window over the kitchen sink.

"Probably." She didn't want to admit how bad she felt when she slowed down. Keeping busy had always somehow helped her outpace the darkness she feared would consume her one day.

"Makes sense." He set his palms on the counter. "I'm not one for sticking around in one place too long, either. Especially not here in Jacobstown."

"Why is that, Jordan Kent?" She had an idea. "You love your family. They all live here. Why is it that you won't?"

He shrugged his shoulders. "Always felt hemmed in here."

The front door opened, and Courtney felt exposed. Before she could excuse herself, Deacon and Amber walked into the kitchen. Deacon was third born out of the five brothers. Jordan was the closest in age to Amber, her being the baby of the family.

"Welcome home, Jordan," Deacon and Amber said almost simultaneously.

Jordan greeted his siblings with a hug, and Courtney couldn't help but admire the closeness of the Kent siblings. Once again, she was reminded what a tight-knit and loving bunch they were. And, again, she realized her hand rested on her stomach.

"You guys remember Courtney Foster, right?" Jordan said to his sister and brother.

"How could I forget one of my own friends?" Amber said with a side glance toward her brother as she walked over and embraced Courtney in a warm hug.

Deacon smiled and cocked one eyebrow as he took in her outfit. "I'd heard you came back to town and went to work for Zach. Welcome home."

"It's good to be here." It wasn't exactly a lie. She'd wanted to return to her hometown but coming back to the Jacobstown Hacker hadn't been her ideal homecoming.

"Courtney stayed over in the guest room last night after practically freezing out on the property. I bumped into her and asked her to stay here instead of driving home." Jordan was overexplaining, but she appreciated him leaving no room for speculation as to why she was in the house with him so early in the morning wearing her pj's.

Thankfully, he'd thrown on a T-shirt at some point, which also most likely meant he hadn't slept.

"We got your message this morning and were hoping to catch you," Amber said to her brother. She must be talking about the text he'd told Courtney about sending to his siblings earlier to warn them about going out alone.

"I'm happy to see the two of you together and no one walking around by themselves. It's strange to think we have to be so careful on our own property." Jordan filled all of them in on his conversation with their cousin.

Courtney expected a few strange looks from Amber and Deacon, but their faces were impossible to read. Courtney and Amber had lost touch after high school. It struck her as odd that she was at the Kent house with Amber's brother.

A wave of nausea hit fast and hard. "I'm sorry. Please excuse me for one second."

She didn't have time to glance at any of them to judge a reaction. All she could think about was getting to the bathroom in time. She barely made it to the washroom before what little she'd had to eat came back up.

A few rounds of dry heaves later, she rinsed out her mouth and brushed her teeth. She actually felt a little better.

Her stomach gurgled and groaned, but this time for a different reason. Hunger took over.

A knock on the bathroom door startled her.

"Are you okay in there?" Jordan's deep baritone washed over her, providing more comfort than she wanted to acknowledge.

"Better." She opened the door to find him leaning against the jamb. "Thanks for checking."

"I brought a bottle of water just in case." He held out the offering, and she took it. Their fingers grazed as a jolt of electricity shot through her.

It was probably just hormones causing her body

to overreact to his presence. She needed to get a handle on this out-of-control chemistry. She'd thought about that kiss first thing this morning. Knowing it had been a bad idea and still wishing for a repeat meant she was heading down the wrong path.

"Thanks for this." She took a sip. "I'll be right out."

He disappeared, closing the bedroom door behind him.

She dressed in fresh clothes—yoga pants and a pullover sweater. This was one of her most comfortable outfits, and she'd almost forgotten about it being there after all that had gone on so far that morning.

Taking in a fortifying breath, she walked into the next room. A dozen thoughts fought for attention. She couldn't help but wonder what Amber and Deacon truly thought about her being there. Had she and Jordan given themselves away?

How long had it been since she'd been in this house?

A rogue thought struck. How was Amber going to take the pregnancy news? More panic shot through Courtney. Before Jordan could talk her out of leaving, she had to get out of there.

She moved into the kitchen, rounded up her belongings and gave an awkward wave to the trio.

"I forgot about an appointment I made for this

morning. I'm going to be late if I don't leave right now."

Jordan shot a look and seemed about to say something when she darted toward the front door and closed it behind her.

THANKFULLY, HER VEHICLE had been brought to the main house for her. Jordan must've made the arrangements last night when she was sleeping. Courtney figured she could run a few errands while Jordan gathered his family together to come up with a plan for more patrols along Rushing Creek. She'd slept in this morning, and physically felt better than she had in weeks.

The idea of a pregnancy might not be growing on her, exactly, but she was a little less freaked about it. Although she was a long way from thinking it was a good idea. Seeing Jordan being protective of her and the little bean had warmed her heart.

The first spark of the two of them actually being able to co-parent was starting to ignite. She was beginning to feel like she might not be a complete disaster as a mother or totally mess up the child before he or she got a start in life. Was it weird that she didn't have becoming a mother as part of her trajectory? Was it strange that she'd never really thought of herself as parent material?

Part of the reason she figured she'd been so

attracted to Decks was his aversion to ever getting married again and the fact that he already had a child from his first marriage. Courtney had thought he'd be safe. And she'd loved him, right? Granted, she and Decks had never had the same spark she'd experienced with Jordan, but there was more to a relationship than smoking-hot chemistry.

Courtney drove through her bank's ATM line, picked up a few supplies at the grocery store and then stopped by her house to check the mail. She ate more yogurt—this time it stayed down—before changing into slacks. She kept her favorite pullover sweater on while she wrangled her hair into a ponytail.

Some of her best ideas came when she wasn't overthinking a case. She made a mental note to follow up on what had happened with Lopez's interview with Gus Stanton. Granted, she hadn't lived in Jacobstown in years, but her sweet elderly neighbor had. Courtney made another mental note to talk to Mrs. Farmer. Over the years, someone had to have had a foot get caught in a tractor blade or lawn mower. What other incidents could there have been? She thought way back to her earliest memories. Hadn't there been a kid who got his foot stuck in playground equipment? She remembered something about him—what was his name? John Michael?—ending up with a shattered ankle. Didn't he walk with a limp afterward? And being in the country, there had to have been a kid who'd pranked another friend with fireworks, and that could've easily gotten out of control. A foot could've been lost that way. There had to have been a decent list of teen antics that could have led to problems with a left foot.

Within half an hour, she'd charged her phone, logged on to her laptop and paid her electric bill, and freshened up her face with a little makeup. Jordan had texted with an invite to dinner, and she was debating whether or not it was a good idea to go.

On the one hand, it was dinner she didn't have to cook. That was always a plus. For another, having company to eat with sounded wonderful. She'd told him that she'd text him with an answer. Her finger hovered over the cell's keypad.

Eating with Jordan wouldn't be the worst thing that could happen to her. Besides, it was good for the two of them to practice getting along. A small part of her wished for a real family for her child. But she and Jordan could be the next closest thing. A child could do worse than two parents who got along.

Thinking of her unborn child, Courtney pulled the business card of a counselor that she'd been given by one of her colleagues after the shooting. Officer Ralph Howard had been discreet when he'd slipped the worn business card into her palm during a handshake when she'd returned to work after recovering from being shot. He'd leaned in and said, "I've used her when the job got to be too much. She knows her stuff and, more importantly, she knows how to keep private conversations private. She lost her husband to the job. She knows what the pressure is like."

Maybe it was time to think about setting up a phone appointment. Talking couldn't hurt. Right? If Courtney didn't like what she heard in the first five minutes, she could always end the appointment and hang up. She almost laughed out loud. Cops were distrustful by nature. She couldn't even trust a person whose life's work was helping people exactly like Courtney. Having an exit plan, though, eased some of the anxiety that came with the thought of opening up to a complete stranger about the intimate details of her mind, of the feeling of being judged for her thoughts.

Panic climbed up her throat like a vine, squeezing, choking out her oxygen. She gasped and brought her hand to her neck as if it was real.

She paced as questions swirled in her mind with the relentless pursuit of a stalker.

Courtney would normally distract herself with an intense workout, but she was concerned that might hurt the baby. Without talking to her doctor, she figured it best to lay off pushing her body to the point of dripping-with-sweat exhaustion. Besides, her stomach was calm for the moment, and she didn't want to stir up that hornet's nest again. She had a monthly OB appointment and no reason to push it up. Nausea was the absolute worst. It was a slow drain on the system to feel sick all day long. Courtney didn't wish the feeling on her worst enemy.

Frustration nipped at just how much her life was changing and just how out of control everything seemed. Coming home to Jacobstown was supposed to provide a respite. It was supposed to nurture her tortured soul but was becoming a mental prison instead. Wow, had she just described her life and her pregnancy as a mental prison?

Deep down, she didn't feel that way at all. She picked up the business card again and ran her index finger along the embossed name, Dr. Sara Winters.

The call could wait until she ran one more errand. Blue Trunks had been bugging her, and her mind was spinning out. The guy most likely had nothing to do with Jacobstown or the jerk terrorizing its citizens.

There was only one way to try to find him and that was to return to The Mart and wait him out.

THE FRONT DOORKNOB TURNED, catching Jordan off guard. He thought Deacon and Amber had locked it when they left. On instinct, Jordan went for the shotgun tucked above the kitchen cabinet far out of reach of little hands but easy enough to access in an emergency.

Five rapid taps confirmed Lone Star Lonnie was about to walk through the door. Jordan abandoned his attempt to snatch the shotgun and started toward the door. A sheet-white-faced Lonnie stared at Jordan.

"What's wrong?" he asked.

Lone Star's face twisted and he issued a sharp sigh.

"You need to come and take a look at what's on the porch," Lone Star said.

"What is it?" Jordan's pace quickened, making double time.

"A foot."

Chapter Eight

Jordan rushed outside and stopped dead in his tracks when he saw the freezer bag on the first step leading up to the porch.

"It's human," he said to Lonnie. "Small in size with painted toenails."

He fished his cell from his pocket and called Zach.

"What's going on?" Zach asked.

"You need to get over to the ranch as soon as possible. There's either a really sick prank on my porch steps or *he's* been here," Jordan said.

"I'm on my way now. I'm not far." Zach's rapid breathing told Jordan that his cousin had started sprinting. "What is it?"

"It looks like a female's foot," Jordan supplied.

Zach muttered a string of curses. "You already know this, but don't touch anything."

"I won't." The two stayed on the line until Zach arrived fifteen minutes later.

Zach took a statement from Lone Star Lonnie. Jordan gave his, which was little more than what he'd already told his cousin. He looked from one to the other when he said, "I'd like to keep this finding quiet. This guy is taunting us, and I don't want to tip my hand just yet."

"No one outside of this property will hear any of this from me." Jordan had every intention of telling his siblings and their spouses. The security team and ranch hands deserved to know, as well. Other than that, Jordan was fine with keeping the news on the ranch.

"We interviewed and cleared the staff last year. No one new has been hired since then. Still, I'd like to interview the staff again. Someone might've seen something." Zach was following protocol, Jordan knew that. His cousin snapped photos of the bottom step where the evidence was found and the surrounding area.

"They might have questions. You're the best one to give answers," Jordan said to his cousin.

Deputy Lopez's SUV wound up the path. Zach brought the evidence over to him and sent him away with it.

"I told him to request a rush on DNA testing," Zach said to Jordan. Breanna Griswold's death stared them in the face, and there were still more theories than evidence. The jerk responsible for killing Breanna still walked the streets. And Jordan could only hope the man had made his first mistake.

"You want to come in for a cup of coffee while Lone Star rounds up the staff?" Jordan asked.

"Sounds like a good plan," Zach said.

Lone Star broke off, and Zach followed Jordan into the kitchen.

After filling coffee mugs, Jordan joined his cousin at the granite island in the kitchen where everyone usually gathered.

"If the DNA matches Breanna's, he kept her body part preserved." Zach punched in a few letters on the keypad of his cell phone.

"Why would he do that?" Jordan had no idea how the criminal mind worked.

"Keeping a 'souvenir' is a way to relive the experience of the crime over and over again until he or she is able to satisfy the next urge." Zach leaned back in his chair and pinched the bridge of his nose. "There might be another scenario going on here."

"A threat?" All Kent women were accounted for as of this morning. Jordan had already reached out to his brothers and sister.

"It could be a twisted gift, a warning message." Zach picked up a pen and rolled it around his fingers. "Or that bastard might be taunting us."

"He got past ranch security. He knows the area, which makes me think he's been watching our every move," Jordan stated. "How? Who could be that crafty without any of us knowing it?"

"As an investigator, I'd normally look more closely at the family and staff." The pen flipped out of his grip, crashing onto the desk. "But you guys are my family. I know that a Kent would never do anything remotely like this. And the staff on the ranch boils down to Lone Star Lonnie and a handful of his devoted guys. Then there's Kimberly, Mitch's wife. Our perp is most likely male. The person who killed Breanna is either tricky or strong, most likely both. She was five feet six inches and weighed 140 pounds at the time of her death. There was no sign of struggle, which would indicate she knew her attacker, but the few people she'd been around that day have alibis. I've had no break in this case. Now citizens are scared and reporting missing people to the tune of half a dozen a day."

"What if someone has gone high-tech with their spying?" It was probably a long shot, but every idea was fair game at this point.

"As in someone put a camera on the property?" Zach asked.

"Could be on the property. Could be using a drone. Hell, the camera could be across the street zooming in on us right now for all I know," Jordan pointed out.

"Those are valid points." Zach jotted a few

notes. "We haven't looked at this from the angle of someone targeting a Kent specifically."

"Our land is vast, and you said a while ago there were reports of dead animals on other ranches in the area. None of us thought this was a specific threat to us. With the clock ticking, it's time to look at this from all angles." Jordan smacked the granite with his flat palm.

"How's Courtney?" Zach didn't look up, so he wasn't trying to gauge Jordan's reaction to the question. It was probably innocent enough and not an indication that Zach had caught on to the relationship going on between the two of them.

"She seemed better the last time I saw her," Jordan said, noncommittal.

"I spoke to Deacon, and he said she stayed over at the main house last night after checking an area near Rushing Creek," Zach said.

"That's right. She was on the property late, and I bumped into her. She was cold, so I convinced her to come inside and eat."

Zach's eyebrow shot up, but to his credit he didn't say anything.

"It was late," Jordan added by way of explanation. "She was too tired to drive home."

"Amy has been worried about Courtney. Said she's been trying to reach Courtney without any luck," Zach continued. "Did she mention anything to you?"

Jordan shook his head. He could only hope his family wouldn't put two and two together and figure him and Courtney out before he had a chance to convince her that keeping the pregnancy secret would only cause hurt feelings later. He understood that she was gun-shy when it came to spreading the news too early. She'd only just found out and, by way of luck, so had he. It would take a minute for her to digest the surprise and get comfortable talking about their situation.

"If you cross paths—"

"I doubt I'll see her before you do." Jordan's quick rebuke must've sent up a red flag, because Zach stopped what he was doing and studied Jordan. "If I do, though, I'll be sure to tell her that Amy's on the hunt."

Zach laughed. *On the hunt* was the way they used to refer to Amy when she was looking for anyone who'd frustrated her. It was good to break the tension, and, besides, Jordan needed to change the direction of the conversation. If any one of his family members caught on that there was more going on between him and Courtney than courtesy and concern, and asked outright, he already knew that he wouldn't lie about their relationship. That much was a given. But he'd made a promise not to voluntarily spill the beans, and his word could be counted on.

Before his cousin could dig any deeper, Jordan

ended the conversation by asking, "Will you let me know when the forensics results come back? I'd like to know what we're dealing with as soon as the information is available."

"You know I will, Jordan. Even with a rush request, it might take time." Zach's cell buzzed. He checked the screen. It was Ellen. "I better take this."

Zach put the call on speaker.

"Excuse me, Sheriff," she started right in.

"What's going on?" Zach asked.

"I just took a call from Liesel at the diner. She had to get off the phone pronto because she came back from her lunch break to find Reggie Barstock walking out the front door. She was afraid he'd come back inside when he saw her. He had a to-go bag in his hands," Ellen said.

Zach's expression dropped, and his lips thinned. "She say which way he was headed or what kind of vehicle he was driving?"

"She said he was in an older model white sedan." Ellen issued a sharp sigh. "Do you want me to send a deputy to speak to her?"

"I'd rather have them drive the area instead," Zach instructed. "Did she say there was anything different about his appearance?"

"He was wearing a red bandana on his head is all she said," Ellen informed. "And she said he still had that limp."

"Ask Lopez to take the call. He's the closest to the diner. Recirculate the picture of Barstock with the request and let everyone know to be on the lookout for him." Zach glanced at Jordan, who was relieved for the change in subject.

"Yes, sir," Ellen said before ending the call.

The timing of Barstock being seen when a severed foot in a plastic freezer bag showed up on the Kent property was interesting. But what could Reggie Barstock have against the Kent family? They didn't know him or his mother all that well, as far as Jordan knew. He made a mental note to ask his family at dinner tonight what the possible connection could be if there was one.

He also thought about Courtney.

Jordan figured this was a good time to redirect the visit.

"Do you need me to come down to the barn with you while you speak to the men?" he asked.

"No. I'm fine on my own," Zach said.

"There's a hefty amount of work waiting for me." And he wanted to get in touch with Courtney. Too many thoughts rolled around in his mind, and he was tempted to call Courtney the minute Zach got out the door.

Jordan fished his phone out of his front pocket and thought about what he might say. He figured she wouldn't take lightly to feeling like he was checking up on her. She'd always had an independent streak wider than the Texas sky.

He tried to convince himself that he was concerned for the child and not her. He didn't want to care about Courtney so much that he missed her the second she was gone. Courtney or anyone else, for that matter.

Jordan pulled up her name in his contacts anyway. His thumb hovered over her name.

COURTNEY SAT IN her parked car at the south end of the parking lot of The Mart, where she had the best vantage point. Here, she could see vehicles coming and going. Most people repeated the same patterns, so she figured Blue Trunks would park in or near the same parking spot as the last time if he returned.

It was a long shot that he'd come back on the same day she chose to stake out the lot, but she had to do something. It never hurt to take a chance. Sometimes, rolling the dice paid off. Kids were still at school. The Mart was overrun by cars. She usually liked to avoid big-box stores because it seemed like everyone in town came out at the same time. The aisles were cramped, and the people were cranky. Courtney wasn't one for shopping anyway. Those conditions made it even less pleasant.

After an hour, she started rethinking her judgment call on staking out The Mart. It was her day off, and she was becoming obsessed with the case. An annoying little voice in the back of her head tried to tell her that she was fixated on this case because she had a chance to solve it. Because of the one she couldn't go back and fix. What justice could she bring to the families of the eight officers who were shot dead while she was spared?

Her heavy thoughts were interrupted by the sight of a pickup that fit the description of Blue Trunks'. It was probably a long shot and not the right vehicle, but she watched it circle the parking lot. It stopped in front of the double glass sliding doors of the entrance and then made another lap. No one got in the vehicle from what she could tell at this distance.

She started the engine and kicked up the heater a couple of notches. In the last hour or so, the temperature had dipped again to a chilly forty-five degrees. It was midday and the sun was out, which was her saving grace. The vehicle had stayed fairly warm inside, especially with her long coat on, but her hands were like ice. She gripped the steering wheel and tailed the older pickup as it pulled out of the parking lot.

The pickup pulled onto Riverside Lane, which was a main thoroughfare through Bexford. Courtney had to stay far enough back so as not to draw attention to herself. From her position thirty feet behind, she could see there was no passenger in the vehicle.

The driver made a left-hand turn. Courtney tried to get a look, but all she could see clearly was that the driver wore some kind of cap, maybe a baseball cap. She slowed her pace and then made the same turn.

The vehicle was gone. A moment of panic set in. She scanned the parking pads as she drove through the neighborhood of white cottage-style homes from around the 1920s. The neighborhood road was barely big enough for one lane with cars parked on both sides of the street and on parking pads. Wire fences encased the front and backyards.

Courtney rolled her window down halfway to listen. Other than dogs barking, trying to hop the fence and chase her, there was no sign of life or hint of the vehicle. People in Texas didn't do cold weather, so there were no young kids playing in the yards while older siblings attended school. In fact, there was surprisingly little activity. She sped up a little bit, checking side streets as she passed them by.

After the fourth one, she saw it. The pickup turned right. So Courtney sped up in order to catch it. She followed as it weaved through cars in the neighborhood.

If this went on much longer, she'd be made. At the time it was about get pretty obvious that she was following, the pickup pulled onto a parking pad. Courtney pulled behind a blue Mustang but kept the ignition in Drive, just in case. She picked up her cell and turned on the camera feature.

The driver came around the front of the pickup. And then Courtney got a good look at *her*. It was a woman and not Carolina Blue Trunks. Courtney waited for the woman to go inside her front door before she slipped out of her spot and headed back toward home.

Staking out The Mart while not on official duty wasn't the smartest idea. *What if* she had found Carolina Blue Trunks? Then what? She had no reason to talk to him, and she wasn't driving an official vehicle because she didn't want to scare him off in the event he saw her. She had no backup out here.

Courtney navigated her way onto the highway. Her cell rang, and she answered it over the vehicle's speaker.

"What did you decide about dinner?" Jordan's voice came through clearly. His masculine tone sent warmth vibrating through her, warming places she knew better than to allow.

"I should probably stay home tonight," she said without much enthusiasm. The thought of going home alone and wrestling those nightmares again was about as appealing as eating a heated can of soup for dinner. Sure, it got the job done, but that was about it.

"Zach asked me about you earlier."

"What did you say?" She couldn't hide the moment of panic in her tone.

"Nothing that he didn't already know. He spoke to my family. Speaking of which, Amy is looking for you." There was no hint of judgment in those words.

"I know. I haven't had a chance to return her call yet. Besides, I'm at a loss as to what to say to anyone right now," she admitted.

"If you don't want to come to dinner, can I swing by your place? We need to talk." Those last four words she'd been half expecting and mostly dreading.

"Think we could do it another day?" She didn't want to see him while she was feeling so vulnerable and alone. This was the time to armor up, not run toward enemy lines. But was he the enemy? An annoying little voice in the back of her head questioned. Logically, she knew he wasn't the problem. It was her. Being in his arms last night had felt a little too right, and it was a foreign feeling. No man had made her feel as safe and cherished as Jordan. And their relationship had been temporary. She'd known it would be going in.

"It's important." He'd armored up, too. But he wasn't giving an inch, and that had her concerned.

"I'm not up for another round of negotiations on when we should tell people about the pregnancy, if that's what you need to discuss." She needed to be clear on that point. The topic was closed for now.

"It's not." She picked up on the hurt—and maybe frustration?—in those two words.

"Okay. I'd rather come to your place then." It would be easier to leave when she was ready to wrap up the conversation that way. It gave her the illusion of having control over how the evening went.

"What time can you be here?" he asked.

"I can head that way now, if you're home." Better face this conversation and get it over with than dread it for the rest of the day.

"Now's good."

Chapter Nine

"Come in," Jordan said to Courtney as she stood on the same step the severed foot was found on. Jordan looked across the vast yard. He'd never given much thought to security growing up at KR. As a child, he'd been able to run free without a care.

"I can't stay long." Courtney walked inside but stood in the foyer. She didn't take her coat off, and he wondered if she was embarrassed about the kiss from last night. He'd thought about it more than he wanted to during the course of the day.

"Are you sure?" he asked.

"How much do you have to tell me?" Her beautiful eyes stared at him. She had the kind of eyes that sparked and drew him in. Her thick curly hair was pulled away from her heart-shaped face and too-pink lips.

"It's not the quantity of words," he warned.

"What happened?" She took in a breath and

shrugged out of her coat. He took it from her and hung it in the hall closet.

Jordan led her into the kitchen, where he offered her a bottle of water. He watched as she took a seat at the granite island and then unscrewed the cap. She set the bottle on the hard, shiny surface without taking a sip.

"First, someone left what looks like a severed and frozen female foot on the porch earlier today," he started.

"When? I was here. I didn't see anything, Jordan."

"Lone Star Lonnie found it sometime after Deacon and Amber left." He poured a cup of coffee for himself before joining her at the island. "Also, you'll find this out when you go back to work tomorrow, but Reggie Barstock was sighted at the diner by an employee."

She immediately stood. "I need to be out there looking for him."

"It's your day off, Courtney. And I didn't tell you any of this so you'd run out of here and try to solve this yourself—"

"Either way, I should be out there helping instead of in here." Her eyes searched the room, and she looked flushed. There was a desperate quality to her voice that was a gut punch.

"Zach's involved, and we're having a family meeting over dinner. Staying here might do more good than being out there where you have nothing to go on." He paused—knowing when it was time to stop and not oversell an idea was important. "I'd like to see if anyone here can think of any reason Reggie Barstock might do something like that or if anyone's connected to him or his mother in any way other than Chelsea. Living in Idaho, I'm not always aware of the day to day here in Texas. But they are, and if they've had any interaction with Barstock, we'll know it."

"Didn't one of your sisters-in-law inherit his mother's home and business?" she asked.

"As a matter of fact, my brother's wife, Chelsea, was given the family home and business downtown," he said.

"She's married to Nate, if memory serves. When did she move here?"

"It's been a couple of months now. They've been married for a few weeks. Reggie wasn't thrilled about his mother leaving her home to Chelsea, who is her great-niece, and he pulled a few stunts to try to scare her into leaving. But the animal killings started before that," Jordan said.

"That's true. I see why all roads keep leading back to Reggie, but the evidence isn't as clear cut. He would have motive if he felt slighted by his mother and wanted to get back at the people who benefited. He could see your family as part of the problem," she stated. "He was always quiet, troubled, which is most likely why his mother cut her only son out of her will in the first place. When I spoke to Mrs. Porter the other morning, she said he wasn't stupid. She wouldn't exactly classify him as the smartest kid in class, but he held his own."

"He didn't have a relationship with his mother toward the end of her life, and he's been in and out of jail for small crimes," Jordan said.

"Serial killers don't normally work up from the kinds of crimes Reggie is known for. And, also, they rarely get caught, especially one as meticulous as the one we're dealing with." Courtney picked up a pen and started clicking it.

"Those are good points. I also keep questioning, why Breanna? How does she fit into the puzzle? She wasn't exactly friends with my sister or Amy," he said.

"From what I remember, Breanna didn't have a lot of friends. She was his first human kill that we know of." The corners of Courtney's lips turned down in a frown. "She might've been an easy mark. We know she was using again, and that could have left her vulnerable if she passed out somewhere in public. An easy mark might not be as exciting, but we know that there was no sexual abuse with her. There were no signs that she fought back. My guess is that he moved quickly."

"It seems like he'd be crazy to stick around Jacobstown. He has to know everyone has been *and* will be looking for him. If he's part of the community in some way, he has to know about all the task forces that have been put together and neighborhood watches," Jordan pointed out.

"That can be part of the thrill for a sicko like him," she said. "I followed a pickup away from The Mart earlier. I was coming home when you called. *If*, and it's a big if, he's responsible, he lives close enough to access the community without actually living here day to day."

Courtney's cell phone buzzed. She fished it out of her purse and checked the screen. "Gus Stanton was just picked up after he tried to ditch his vehicle and run after a routine traffic stop. He assaulted Deputy Lopez, who was able to subdue him. Lopez then found duct tape and rope in this trunk. They're processing Stanton's vehicle to see if there's any DNA in there."

She made a move to retrieve her coat, and Jordan was right behind her. "We can ride in my car."

"You sure about that?" he asked.

"Oh. Right. It might be best if we arrive in separate vehicles." She flashed grateful brown eyes at him, and he took a hit to the center of his chest.

COURTNEY HAD ALMOST blown it by offering to show up to work in the same vehicle as Jordan. She'd have to be more careful moving forward. At least for a few weeks until they could announce the pregnancy.

She thought about her next doctor's appointment and the counseling appointment that would follow. Her child deserved to have a mother who could work through any mental blocks.

Courtney left the house and realized when she got to the car that she'd been touching her stomach again. As much as she didn't want to admit it, she was starting to accept—enjoy?—having the little bean grow inside her. It was more than the morning sickness, but she detected changes in her—and not just ones in her body.

She hadn't started gaining any weight. And, sure, there were bags underneath her eyes that she played off as from food poisoning. She was starting to notice changes in her skin, especially certain places on her face that were dry, while other spots were suddenly oily. She was starting to wish she'd paid more attention to her pregnant former coworkers. She'd tuned out all the office chatter when she'd had to be in the station.

Ready or not, a baby was coming later this year. Which made her think about the phone number on her desk at home. She'd call the counselor first thing tomorrow before her shift.

Although, with recent developments to the biggest case in Jacobstown's history, Courtney figured she'd be working overtime alongside the rest of the department until this jerk was behind bars.

She texted Zach to let him know that she was on her way in to the office. She, like many, wanted to hear firsthand what excuse Gus Stanton had for keeping duct tape and rope in his trunk.

Jordan followed her to Zach's office and parked across the lot from her. He didn't immediately get out of his vehicle, and she appreciated him giving her a little space. She walked in and waved to Ellen.

Volunteers were set up in the conference room, so talking freely was a little more challenging. She didn't want someone overhearing something they shouldn't and spreading false information. Fortunately, the door to the conference room was closed as she walked past it.

Having so many in the community willing to help out made law enforcement's job easier. Having citizens organizing neighborhood watches in order to blanket the various areas and keep watch for any suspicious activity was a big help. Sure, there were people who got in the way. Zach grew up in this community and knew who he could trust with information and was able to sort through a lot of the less helpful folks. His history in Jacobstown was a huge benefit in a situation like this. And most folks had the best of intentions.

Law enforcement personnel were trained to

watch for the one who didn't. It was true what she'd told Jordan about the perp showing up in a veiled attempt to help but actually just being there in order to revel in how he or she had fooled everyone, including the people who lived right next door.

Her instincts tried to convince her that Blue Trunks was involved, but she had no evidence to go on. She'd learned a long time ago to put 10 percent stock in instincts and 90 percent in following the evidence.

The killer was getting cocky by delivering that "souvenir" to the Kent family home. Her heart bled for what Breanna's family would have to learn, for what Breanna had endured. The jerk was also showing them clearly that he could breach security on the Kent ranch any time he wanted. Courtney needed to ask Jordan if there was surveillance footage of the house. Why hadn't anyone seen him come or go? Security had been doubled at the ranch. Which brought her to another question—was the Kent family ranch safe?

Courtney joined Zach in the viewing room, standing behind the two-way mirror, studying the occupant. It was dark on her side of the mirror, and there was another off-duty deputy sandwiched inside the small space. Gus Stanton sat across the table in the next room, facing them. He was alone, handcuffed to the solid desk that was bolted to the

Dear Reader,

Your opinions are important to us. So if you'll participate in our fast and free "One Minute" Survey, **YOU** can pick up to four wonderful books that **WE** pay for!

As a leading publisher of women's fiction, we'd love to hear from you. That's why we promise to reward you for completing our survey.

IMPORTANT: Please complete the survey and return it. We'll send your Free Books and Free Mystery Gifts right away. **And we pay for shipping and handling too!** *We pay for EVERYTHING!*

Try **Harlequin® Romantic Suspense** books featuring heart-racing page-turners with unexpected plot twists and irresistible chemistry that will keep you guessing to the very end.

Try **Harlequin Intrigue® Larger-Print** books featuring action-packed stories that will keep you on the edge of your seat. Solve the crime and deliver justice at all costs.

Or TRY BOTH!

Thank you again for participating in our "One Minute" Survey. It really takes just a minute (or less) to complete the survey… and your free books and gifts will be well worth it!

Sincerely,

Pam Powers

Pam Powers
for Reader Service

"One Minute" Survey

GET YOUR FREE BOOKS AND FREE GIFTS!

✓ Complete this Survey   ✓ Return this survey

▶ DETACH AND MAIL CARD TODAY! ▶

1 Do you try to find time to read every day?
☐ YES   ☐ NO

2 Do you prefer stories with suspenseful storylines?
☐ YES   ☐ NO

3 Do you enjoy having books delivered to your home?
☐ YES   ☐ NO

4 Do you find a Larger Print size easier on your eyes?
☐ YES   ☐ NO

YES! I have completed the above "One Minute" Survey. Please send me my Free Books and Free Mystery Gifts (worth over $20 retail). I understand that I am under no obligation to buy anything, as explained on the back of this card.

☐ I prefer Harlequin®
Romantic Suspense
240/340 HDL GNUS

☐ I prefer Harlequin
Intrigue® Larger Print
199/399 HDL GNUS

☐ I prefer BOTH
240/340 & 199/399
HDL GNWG

FIRST NAME   LAST NAME

ADDRESS

APT.#   CITY

STATE/PROV.   ZIP/POSTAL CODE

BUSINESS REPLY MAIL

FIRST-CLASS MAIL   PERMIT NO. 717   BUFFALO, NY

POSTAGE WILL BE PAID BY ADDRESSEE

READER SERVICE

PO BOX 1341

BUFFALO NY 14240-8571

NO POSTAGE
NECESSARY
IF MAILED
IN THE
UNITED STATES

floor. She noticed a pad of paper and a pen on the table in front of him. She realized Zach would sweat Gus out. He'd give him that pen and paper and tell him that he could leave once he wrote down what really happened to Breanna Griswold.

"How long has he been in there?" she asked in a low voice.

"Definitely not long enough," Zach responded.

Gus wasn't more than five feet nine inches, but he was stocky. Most of his former muscle had gone soft, and he had quite the stomach—the kind that looked like he was about to birth a twelve-pack of beer. His complexion was ruddy, and his bulbous nose looked like a clown's. His light-colored hair wrapped his head, the dome of which shined. He wore overalls with a flannel shirt and looked like he'd already started on that twelve-pack.

She didn't need to set eyes on Jordan to recognize the scent of his aftershave when he walked in. She turned and acknowledged him with a small nod from across the room.

He barely glanced at her, and she felt a twinge of regret. He was only honoring the agreement she'd forced him into, and yet it still felt like rejection, still stung. She wanted to blame her pregnancy for her reaction, but it went deeper than that; she couldn't deny it. Oh, sure, maybe she could cover it up in front of others, but her heart free-fell every time he looked at her.

Movement in the interview room caught her attention. Adrenaline surged when she caught sight of Gus stabbing himself with the pen that had been on the table.

She, Deputy Lopez and Zach jumped into action. Zach went in first with Courtney a close second.

"Stop it right there, Gus," Zach demanded in that authoritative voice only law enforcement seemed to possess.

"Stay away from me." Gus's attempts to stab himself in the neck left marks, but he didn't break skin. The fear was that he'd jam it in an eye or through his ear, where he could do a lot more damage.

Gus pushed back from the table and then tried to topple it. When that didn't work, he held the pen out toward them like it was a weapon.

"You don't want to threaten an officer of the law, Gus," Zach warned. "Trust me on that one."

The three of them encircled him. He shifted his head from side to side. Sweat rolled down his forehead.

"No one will believe me that I'm innocent. Not now. The judge will take my kids away. Arresting me for this is the last straw my ex needs to cut me out of my kids' lives forever," Gus shouted. "I might as well have done whatever it is you're accusing me of."

"What do you think you're in here for?" Zach took a step toward Gus, who swiped the pen through the air like it was a knife.

"I know what you think I did. That's sick. I wouldn't do that to another human being," Gus argued. A look of disgust crossed his ruddy features as he focused his attention on Zach, which gave Courtney the opportunity to tackle him from behind. She dived into the back of his knees. Deputy Lopez took a swipe at the pen at the same time she made her move and caught Gus's meaty hand.

Courtney made contact, and Gus flew backward, landing square on top of her. He felt like he weighed two hundred pounds. His elbow caught her in the back as his heft knocked her to the floor. She scrambled to make herself into a ball in order to protect her organs, but it was too late. He was too heavy. So he flattened her like a pancake. Her mind flashed to the little bean growing in her stomach, and she flinched.

Before Gus could strike her or move, he was being lifted off her. She pushed up to all fours in time to see the others, Jordan included, slam Gus facedown onto the hard flooring. Within a few seconds, his hands were pulled hard behind his back and he was in zip cuffs.

Her stomach cramped, and her gaze flew to Jordan, who was studying her. In the next second, he was beside her, righting the chair that had been turned on its side and helping her sit in it.

"I'm fine." She couldn't afford to show signs of weakness in her line of work. She stood and dusted herself off before looking at him. "It's fine."

A muscle pulsed in Jordan's jaw. He clenched his back teeth hard. He, of all people, should understand the position she was in. When it came to doing her job, she had to show that she could pull her weight. Lives of other law enforcement officers depended on her. His gaze was fierce and protective.

"Can I have a word with you in the hall, please?" he ground out, and it look liked he was using an enormous amount of self-control to hold on to what he had to say.

Courtney's gaze flew to her boss, who nodded.

Jordan, who'd witnessed the exchange, started toward the door almost immediately.

In the hallway, Jordan whirled around on her. The intensity of his gaze almost knocked her back a step.

"You have until morning to tell him," he said. "I can't go along with this any longer in good conscience."

"That's too soon," she argued. "I need more time."

Chapter Ten

"No can do." Jordan didn't to take a hard line but Courtney was forcing his hand. He'd just witnessed her in a struggle that could've ended badly for their unborn child.

"I know you're right, Jordan. Once this jerk is put away we can circle back—" Courtney had another think coming if she thought changing the subject would help her argument to keep the pregnancy a secret.

"I won't change my mind about telling Zach tomorrow." Jordan was firm on that point.

She shot him an incredulous look, opened her mouth to speak and then seemed to think better of it as she glanced around. "This isn't the time or the place. We can discuss this matter after dinner tonight when everyone goes home. We'll make a decision then. Deal?"

"No. I'll listen to whatever you have to say, but we've done this your way so far and none of it feels right." Jordan realized she had the most to lose in the equation, and that was the reason he'd agreed to her idea in the first place. But she was putting herself in jeopardy by doing her job when she wasn't at full strength, and he doubted she even realized it or would allow herself to consider the thought. She wasn't a glutton for punishment. He wondered if the cause of the nightmares was the same reason she wasn't thinking clearly now— her past.

There was plenty she could contribute inside the office rather than going out into the field every day. A desk job was better than nothing, and Zach needed plenty of help training and organizing volunteers for neighborhood watches as well as answering the tip line. There was a lot for her to do that didn't involve physical altercations with scumbags.

Zach walked into the hallway before Courtney could mount another defense. "Both of you mind stepping into my office?"

"Not at all," Jordan said with a glance toward Courtney.

Courtney nodded, but a flash of panic crossed her features. He had no intention of rolling her under the bus. He'd told her what his intention was, and he planned to stick to it. Come tomorrow morning, he'd have a conversation with his cousin in confidence. He and Courtney could come up with a plan to tell his family together if that's what she wanted.

"What's going on with you two?" Zach didn't mince words as he closed the door to his office behind the three of them.

"Not anything we want to discuss." Jordan wasn't lying.

Zach shot his cousin a look.

"It's personal. We go way back," Courtney interjected.

"We all go way back, but you can't storm into an interview room like that again, Jordan." Zach's tone left no room for argument. "Courtney's a deputy and a damn fine one. She can handle herself."

"Any chance we can delay this conversation until tomorrow, Zach?" It was an earnest question. By then Zach would understand what Jordan's reaction was about. It would all make sense.

"I've said what I have to say about it." Zach's gaze bounced from Jordan to Courtney. If Zach had figured out there was something going on between them, he didn't let on. Jordan was relieved for Courtney's sake. He wasn't trying to force her hand. He'd hoped that she'd seize the opportunity to speak up, but that seemed to be hoping for too much.

When Courtney shut down, she was a closed book. Her arms folded, she said, "I appreciate your confidence. I'm fully capable of doing my job. I think Jordan was reacting to the fact that I've been under the weather lately."

"Food poisoning?" Zach asked.

"That's right."

"And that's the story you're comfortable telling?" Damn. Zach knew something was up.

"It is," she replied. "I'd like to request a meeting with you before my shift in the morning. Just the two of us."

"Have Ellen put it on my calendar." His eyebrow arched.

"Yes, sir," she said.

Jordan figured Courtney was giving herself the night to talk him out of making the announcement to the people he cared about. There was no amount of cajoling that could turn that into reality.

"I'll see you tonight at dinner, Jordan. Okay?" she asked.

BY THE TIME Courtney woke after her long nap, it was dark outside. She freshened up before checking her phone. Amy had called again. Courtney let her thumb hover over Amy's name. One tap and Amy would be on the line.

What would Courtney say to her former friend? To any Kent relative? The thought of sitting across the dinner table from Jordan's family kicked off a whole reaction in her body.

She tucked her phone inside her purse instead.

A wave of guilt struck as Courtney strapped on her shoulder holster. The annoying voice in the back of her mind returned. What was the point of friendships when everyone she'd cared about at one time was dead now?

Was that really true? She knew she was being irrational. Instead of fighting it, she resolved to make the call to the counselor. Right now, it was time to face the music—the Kent family.

Before she made it to the door, a knock sounded. Panic heated her veins.

She reminded herself to breathe.

After checking the peephole, Courtney opened the door to a frantic-looking Mrs. Farmer. A cold gust of wind slammed into Courtney. It was five forty-five in the evening and already dark in Jacobstown.

"Sassy got out of the yard." The woman was pushing seventy-five and loved her Yorkshire terrier more than anything. "You know there've been coyotes in the neighborhood lately, and I'm scared one will get to her."

Sassy had a habit of slipping underneath the fence. Courtney was almost convinced the little pooch did it for attention. Sassy had a flair for the dramatic.

Of course, Mrs. Farmer could've left the front door open for the mental state she'd been in. She'd walked next door and introduced herself on Court-

ney's first morning in her newly rented bungalow-
style home. Mrs. Farmer had cooked a southwest
skillet breakfast and brought it over, still steaming.
It was the best first morning Courtney had spent
anywhere but the cabin with Jordan. No amount
of eggs and vegetables could top those seven days.
But the offering had been the closest thing in recent memory. She didn't even want to think about
those nights.

"I'm sure we can find her." Courtney grabbed
her cell phone out of her purse and put on her belt.
She met Mrs. Farmer on the porch. The woman
had a full head of gray hair that she wore in messy
bun. She was as tall as Courtney and had the clear-
est green eyes. She carried herself elegantly, like
she was former royalty. Mr. Farmer had passed
away six months ago, and Mrs. Farmer seemed to
be in the thick of the grieving process. She never
would've left Sassy outside long enough for the
little Yorkie to get out of the fence in her right
state of mind.

Mrs. Farmer stood on the porch, twisting her
hands together and shivering.

"Let's get a coat on you." Courtney grabbed an
extra warm one from the closet nearest the door
and then set down her phone in order to help. "You
can't go out in those slippers and help find Sassy."

"You're probably right. I didn't have my head

on straight. I saw you turning off lights and worried I'd miss you," she said.

Courtney pulled out a pair of boots from her closet. "Think these will work?"

Mrs. Farmer put them on. "They're a little big, but they'll do fine. We better get out there."

"Did you lock your place up?" Courtney asked.

"Yes, ma'am." Mrs. Farmer pulled a set of keys from her pants pocket.

"Good girl." The last time Sassy got out, she'd run into the field across from the cul-de-sac. It had been daylight and much easier to find her. "Let's start looking in the last place we found her."

"Thank you, Courtney. You can't know how much your help means to me. I'm sorry to be such a bother," the older woman said.

"You're not. Besides, I have a few minutes to spare." She didn't. She was due for dinner at Jordan's house and this would make her late, but she wouldn't tell Mrs. Farmer that or deny helping the woman. As far as neighbors went, Mrs. Farmer was the sweetest. She was like the grandmother Courtney never had.

Courtney locked up her own house and walked out of the cul-de-sac and to the neighboring field with Mrs. Farmer. The elderly woman called for her dog while Courtney trained her flashlight around to various spots on the ground and made kissing noises.

The wind blew, making it difficult to hear movement. Courtney stepped along the field, keeping near the street that led out of the neighborhood. She lived on the outskirts of town and closer to the Kent property than she'd realized when she rented the place.

Of course, finding a rental property in Jacobstown wasn't exactly easy. Most people owned their homes and had lived in them for decades, unlike in Dallas, where it wasn't uncommon to move every few years.

There was also a distinct lack of apartments in Jacobstown, being a small community. There was no motel within the city limits. If someone wanted lodging, they had to find a place up on the highway. There weren't a lot of transients in the area, and most people knew each other and went way back. It was the kind of town people brought up families in.

Courtney made more kissing noises. Activity to her left, deeper into the field caught her attention. She shined her flashlight in the area until she found the culprit, a raccoon. She tried to shoo it away. "Get out of here."

The raccoon stood on its back legs and hissed at her. Courtney tried to discourage it from coming closer by shining her flashlight directly at the creature. All she managed to do was annoy it. Rather than get into a real estate debate with a furry four-legged creature, Courtney decided it was time to move on. She located the biggest stick she could find and palmed it in case the raccoon had any ideas about stalking her.

Courtney kept searching, praying she wouldn't find Sassy in the jaws of a wild animal. For someone who lived in the country, Courtney was most definitely not comfortable out in the woods with animals at night.

The sounds of Mrs. Farmer's voice echoed with the wind from a little farther away than Courtney had intended to separate.

"Come on, Sassy," Courtney pleaded twenty minutes later with no sign of the little dog. Her cell was blowing up with texts. She checked the screen and realized Jordan was worried about her. She sent a text to let him know that she was running late. She hadn't meant to make him stress, and she realized after what had happened at his cousin's office earlier that's exactly what would happen.

She was still trying to wrap her mind around making the announcement to key people in the morning. It wasn't until she saw that fierce protective look in his eyes at the sheriff's office that she realized just how difficult this whole ordeal might be for him. In the last forty-eight hours, since finding out about the pregnancy, she hadn't thought about the impact this news would have on Jordan or his world, or about the position she was putting him in by asking him to keep quiet.

Nothing in her wanted to tell her boss or the Kent family about the pregnancy yet. For safety's sake, she might have to talk about it earlier than she'd like.

It was high time she listened to his point of view and took it into consideration. It would be good practice, because this was the beginning of many joint decisions that would need to be made about their child. *Their child.* Those were two words she never thought she's be saying out loud.

"Sassy," she said quietly, making more kissing noises. It was probably futile to keep calling out the little dog's name. Sassy never came when she was called except to Mrs. Farmer.

After another bitter cold twenty minutes had passed, Courtney decided to circle back and tell Mrs. Farmer they should check at home in case Sassy had gotten spooked and returned to her yard.

A noise stopped Courtney in her tracks. The hairs on the back of her neck pricked. The feeling that someone was watching her crept over her skin. A snorting sound from deeper in the field at the tree line caught her attention. Her first thought was wolf or coyote, neither of which were good signs for Sassy.

Courtney spun around toward the noise and trained her flashlight in its direction. She drew her weapon and held it alongside the flashlight; the bullet would hit the same target if she had to shoot. Tall weeds swayed in the breeze.

She stared at the rustling weeds, waiting for a wild animal to come pouncing out of them. There was no way she was moving until she knew what the heck she was dealing with. She had no plans to become a late-night snack for a hungry black bear. Rare as they might be in this area of Texas, sightings happened.

Just as Courtney was about to give up and walk away, she heard a familiar yip-sounding bark. It was coming from the direction of the snarls that were now echoing across the field. The beast—whatever *it* was—might be after Sassy.

"Come here, girl." Courtney raced toward the sounds of the yips while surveying the area beyond. Sassy was not getting eaten by some wild animal on Courtney's watch. No, sir.

Unexpected tears flooded her eyes as she pushed closer toward the sound while fighting back the panic that was becoming all too familiar when she was thrust into high-pressure situations.

Her hand trembled so hard she worried she wouldn't be able to get off a clean shot when the time came. Granted, most of the time the presence of a weapon was enough to deter a criminal. That wasn't the point, her mind argued.

The thought almost stopped her in her tracks.

Her career was all she had left, and she'd been stubbornly hanging on to it. Pregnancy aside, she couldn't be selfish. Her coworkers' lives depended on her, and it wouldn't be fair to them if she couldn't come through in a pinch.

Damn. She was going to have to request desk duty tomorrow morning.

Sassy's head popped up, bouncing just higher than the weeds, which meant she was struggling to get through the thicket.

Courtney's nerves were being put to the test as she raced toward the little dog. Tears streamed down her cheeks at the thought of not being able to come through for Mrs. Farmer, for Sassy. Courtney didn't even own a dog, but that didn't stop her heart from beating against her rib cage.

"Come on, Sassy. Run, girl," she coaxed.

The little head with a hot-pink ribbon tied around it like a headband bobbed up and down.

And then Courtney saw the blackest eyes focused on the little dog.

Chapter Eleven

The animal chasing Sassy was the size and girth of a coyote. Based on the intensity with which it was chasing the little Yorkie, the thing was starving.

Frustrated tears slipped out and then a moment of resolve—like a flash that rocketed through her body—steeled Courtney. Her grip around her Glock steadied, and she took aim.

"Go away. Get out of here," Courtney screamed at the top of her lungs. She made herself seem bigger by flapping one of her arms, and when that didn't stop the animal's momentum, she shone her flashlight into the beast's eyes.

The coyote shunned the bright light, turning its face away. Sassy got the break she so desperately needed to get a little bit ahead of her chaser.

Courtney shouted louder this time, "Shoo!"

With the coyote gaining ground on Sassy, Courtney took aim. If Sassy's head bobbed at the wrong time or Courtney's hand trembled when she needed it to be steady, she'd kill the wrong animal.

With a final push, she caught the coyote's gaze in the beam of light. Courtney screamed like a wild banshee.

At the last second, the coyote broke right, and for a moment Courtney worried that it would stalk Mrs. Farmer. Until it made a U-turn and bolted toward the tree line from where it came.

Courtney dropped down to her knees in time to catch a trembling Sassy. She holstered her weapon and set down the flashlight. She picked up the little fur ball and cradled her against her cheek. The dog was hard-core shaking but alive.

"Sweet girl. You're okay. You're going to be fine. I got you." Courtney's heart flooded with warmth, and she burst into tears. It was probably just overwrought hormones, but she kept that little dog against her cheek as several seconds ticked by. She whispered reassurances and tried her level best to collect herself after the ordeal.

The sound of footsteps coming closer forced her out of her reverie.

"I got her. She's safe. Your girl is fine." Courtney sniffed back tears and hurried to her feet.

Mrs. Farmer's warm smile melted what was left of the ice encasing Courtney's heart. These two, Mrs. Farmer and Sassy, had broken through to Courtney, and that gave her hope that others could, too. Others like her growing child. And maybe, someday, she could let a man inside her heart, too. If she did, it would be Jordan.

Courtney handed over the little dog, doing her level best to mask her own emotions at the reunion. Mrs. Farmer held her dog with two hands and nuzzled the little creature.

"Sweet girl. Thank heaven you're safe. What would I do if something happened to you?" The dog's tail wagged hard.

"What do you say we get the two of you back inside?" Courtney said.

"I can't thank you enough for saving my Sassy. She would've frozen to death if she'd been out all night," Mrs. Farmer said. "Let me fix you something to eat. I bet I caused you to miss your supper."

"If I didn't already have plans, I'd take you up on that offer," Courtney said. And she wasn't being polite. She really wanted to spend a little more time with the kind woman who seemed a bit lonely.

"Maybe tomorrow then," Mrs. Farmer offered as they made the trek back to her house.

"Definitely tomorrow," Courtney confirmed. "I'm working, but my dinner break is at seven o'clock. Is that too late?"

"Not at all." Mrs. Farmer practically beamed. She started prattling on about what she might decide to cook, and Courtney wondered if the woman had eaten alone every meal since her husband had passed. Sharing a meal was the least Courtney could do for the sweet old woman.

Courtney walked Mrs. Farmer to her front door.

"Your boots," Mrs. Farmer said before Courtney could say goodbye.

"Keep 'em for now. I can pick them up tomorrow," she said.

"Are you sure? I don't think my feet have ever been so warm. You might need them," she said.

"I have another pair in black," Courtney said with a smile. Seeing Mrs. Farmer and Sassy together again after fearing the worst brought another peek of light into dark places in Courtney's heart. She couldn't remember the last time she'd seen someone love anything that much.

"See you tomorrow then." Mrs. Farmer returned the smile and waved.

"Lock up," Courtney reminded before she walked down the steps of the small concrete porch.

She moved to her vehicle and locked the door once she got inside. The creepy feeling of eyes on her returned, but it was most likely the stress of the situation. She'd had the feeling before. It had stalked her for weeks after the shooting in Dallas. She'd go to the grocery store and feel like someone watched her. She'd try to escape to the movies only to feel like she was part of the show.

Time had made it easier to cope. And that was

about all she'd done in the last year. When she really thought about it like that, her life sounded awful.

Courtney navigated her vehicle onto the farm road that led to the Kent ranch, which was a mere half-hour drive from her place on the outskirts of town. Her heart still beat erratically in her chest, but a sense of calm was starting to come over her the longer she was on the road.

Almost a half hour on the dot later, she pulled up to the guard shack. Isaac stepped out as she rolled down her window.

"I'm here to see Jordan," she said.

"Yes, ma'am. He called ahead. Go on through." He pushed the magic button that made the gates open. He stood watch behind her, and she was reminded of what had happened at the ranch just that morning.

Icy fingers gripped her spine thinking about it. What sort of twisted person delivered a foot to someone's doorstep? In the wake of dealing with the Sassy crisis, Courtney hadn't thought about the case. She had a few choice words for Gus Stanton later.

Before she could park, Jordan came outside and stood on the porch. Was this what it had come to on the Kent ranch? The place that had held so much carefree fun in their youth. The family whose hearts were always open to help someone in need was being stalked.

Courtney stepped out of her vehicle. Seeing Jordan standing there on the front porch wearing a button-down shirt, jeans and boots caused her heart to free-fall with no hope of recovery.

He was strikingly handsome. The kind of handsome that took her breath away and released a thousand butterflies in her stomach.

She glanced down at the first step. "This is the spot."

He confirmed with a nod.

She skipped the first step and then walked the rest. The closer she came to Jordan, the more her heart thundered in her chest. She tried to remind herself that he was just a man, the same man who'd teased her mercilessly when they were kids. He'd called her shrimp-fry for the longest time, and once got so mad at her he told her to go play dot-to-dot with her freckles.

"Thank you for showing up. I wasn't sure if you would," was all he said, and the seriousness in his tone sank her stomach to her toes.

JORDAN HAD WAITED six hours and twenty-seven minutes to say what he needed to Courtney. He'd run over every scenario he could think of in his mind at least twice. He'd thought through every possible argument she could put up. He wasn't trying to be a jerk and he could see that her life was about to be upended even more so than his. Her career would have to slow to a crawl at least for the duration of the pregnancy.

"You want to talk on the porch?" she asked.

In the porchlight, she was even more beautiful, but he refused to let the fact sway what he had to say. What they were going through was bigger than just her career. Although he regretted the impact it would have. Hell, having a baby was bigger than the two of them. Sacrifices were going to have to be made on both sides if they were going to provide the best possible upbringing for the little sprout inside her.

Jordan realized that he hadn't reacted well to the news but now that he'd had some time for it to sink in, he would not allow his child to be caught in the middle of two parents who didn't have their acts together.

The child had nothing to do with that and didn't deserve to be punished.

"Do you mind coming inside?" he asked.

"I don't see anyone's cars. Did I miss everyone?" she asked as she walked past him and through the door he held open for her. The night was cold, and the weather was going to turn even worse before it got better tomorrow.

"No one's here."

"Okay." Courtney took the same seat she had

this morning at the granite island figuring he'd explain in a minute.

"Can I get you something to drink?" He'd offer water or milk, but he didn't want to come off as a jerk because she'd been a die-hard coffee drinker before.

"I'm fine." She looked him straight in the eye, those glittery browns of hers digging deep inside him. She picked up a pen and started clicking it. "What's on your mind, Jordan?"

He shouldn't like the sound of his name rolling off her tongue. He did. The difference between being a man and a hormonal teenager meant he wouldn't act on the chemistry pinging between them.

Click. Click.

"I'm not trying to tell you what to do, Courtney. And I'm not pretending to know more than you do about what's best for you or the pregnancy." He put his hands up, palms out, in the surrender position. "But what I saw today can't be good for either one of you."

"Are you finished?" she asked with patience she didn't normally own as she kept eye contact.

"Not yet. I'd appreciate it if you'd hear me out," he said.

Click. Click. Click.

"I already told you that I can't keep lying to my family. We don't keep secrets from each other, and especially not something this big. And *this* is huge," he continued.

She glanced up at him. Her face was unreadable. He signaled that he wasn't done.

Click. Click. Click. Click. Click.

"Because not telling them and tiptoeing around like we did something wrong is worse than any reaction they could have, and besides, what we decide isn't any of their business anyway," he stated. "We both know they will support us no matter what. And I understand if you're afraid to tell anyone too early. They'll keep the news in the family."

Click. Click. Click. Click. Click. Click. Click.

"Would you put that pen down before you break your fingers clicking it?" He didn't mean to sound frustrated, but he couldn't help himself.

She released her grip on the pen, and it crashed against the granite.

"Are you done, Jordan?"

She studied him, and it felt like she could see right through him.

"Yes," he said.

"Good. Because I'm requesting desk duty tomorrow morning." She said the words like they were as obvious as the nose on her face. He waited for more of a reaction from her, more of the ire he was used to getting when he was pretty darn certain he'd pushed her buttons.

None came.

He must've been standing there with his mouth open, because she issued a grunt and said, "Putting the baby in danger isn't being responsible. I know I can be stubborn, but I see that now. It's not just about me any longer. I never intended to do anything to cause problems with the pregnancy. And I realize that I've been selfish in asking you not to tell your family about the baby. I trust them to keep the news quiet."

If his mouth wasn't agape before, then it sure as hell was now.

"What? I'm not an unreasonable person." She looked up at him, and her cheeks flamed. "Okay, fine. I can be difficult to deal with, but I see the light now. All this has been a lot to take in, and I heard what you said about talking to a counselor, too. I'm thinking about it."

"Is that everything?" he asked.

She flinched like she was preparing to be told how wrong she'd been before.

"Courtney, I'm proud of you. It takes a lot of courage to ask for help." It was all he said, all he needed to say.

The next time she looked up at him, her clear brown eyes were watery. "Thank you for saying that, Jordan. That means a lot coming from you."

"I meant every word. I only wish I'd said it sooner," he said, dropping his voice down low as an ill-timed well of need stirred deep inside him, catching him off guard.

She pushed off the counter and stood. "If that's all you wanted to talk about, I'd better go home and skip dinner. It's been a long day."

He did his level best to mask his disappointment.

"Least I can do is feed you," he offered, not wanting to admit just how much he hoped she'd stay a little while longer.

"No, thanks. I'll figure something out at home." The wall he'd chipped away at just came back up.

COURTNEY WOKE THE next morning before her alarm went off and drank a glass of water. A few table crackers went down easy enough and kept her nausea from overwhelming her. She was learning that a greasy fast-food breakfast sandwich first thing in the morning came back up almost as fast as it went down. But table crackers kept things level. She could work with that knowledge.

She'd tossed and turned last night, thinking about the meeting she was scheduled to have with Zach. Telling her boss that she was pregnant six weeks into a new job wasn't exactly high on her list of great first impressions. And she'd have to face her coworkers with the news soon enough. Anxiety caused her shoulder blades to burn with tension. This was going to be more difficult than she'd imagined—and she'd gone full out with her worst nightmares last night. It was a conversation that had to take place. She didn't have to look forward to it. The fact that Zach already suspected the truth provided some measure of comfort.

At least the weather system had moved through the area, and the temperatures were supposed to warm up to the high fifties or low sixties this afternoon.

Courtney cleaned up after her light breakfast and locked up before heading in to work. The drive felt like it took twice as long. And she saw Jordan's vehicle in the parking lot. Her gaze flew to the driver's seat, but he wasn't there, which meant he was already inside.

There were other cars and trucks, too. Volunteers were starting to show up in droves, and the parking lot was brimming over. It was looking like she'd have her work cut out for her on desk duty.

A pang of guilt nipped at her. She hadn't been completely honest with Jordan last night. A big part of the reason she'd conceded was because of the pregnancy, but she also wanted to make sure she could handle herself out there. A cop with trembling hands who couldn't remain calm anymore was a recipe for someone getting hurt. She was embarrassed that she hadn't put her fellow law enforcement officers first. It was a mistake she couldn't allow herself to make, no matter how much she wanted to stay on the job.

She thought about the card sitting on her computer table. She'd snapped a pic of it before leaving the house this morning. After she spoke to Zach, she'd make the call to the counselor. Baby steps. She could do this if she focused on one step at a time. And then she'd call her old friend Amy.

But first, Zach.

With a sigh, she unbuckled her seat belt and then threw her shoulder into the driver's side door to open it. She shivered against the cold wind. The bright sun reminded her that it would warm up at some point that day.

Courtney badged into the side entrance. She thought about Gus Stanton, who was most likely still in the jail. Now that he'd tried to harm himself, he would need a psych evaluation. He was most likely awaiting transport to a mental facility for further evaluation.

With another deep breath for fortitude, Courtney knocked on her boss's door. She expected to see Jordan sitting in one of the club chairs when she opened the door after he called out to her. Her traitorous heart skipped a beat at the disappointment when she realized her boss was alone. Maybe she'd imagined seeing Jordan's vehicle in the parking lot. It shouldn't surprise her. His cousin was sheriff and many town residents were volunteering. Maybe she was losing her mind from all the recent stress Then, there was the pregnancy. That last part was most believable. She'd definitely been off the past six weeks.

"Morning, Zach," she said to her boss when he looked up from the screen he'd been studying.

"Is it?" His eyes were bloodshot, and he looked like he was wearing the same shirt from yesterday.

"Did you go home last night?" She took the chair closest to the door.

"No."

"I should've come in." She didn't want him holding the bag.

"You're still recovering from food poisoning, remember? And it was your day off," he pointed out.

"It wasn't food poisoning, Zach. I took a test. It was positive." She put her hand on her stomach. "Jordan is the father."

Chapter Twelve

Zach studied Courtney before he responded, and she realized he was searching for a clue from her as to whether this was good news or bad news, or she expected him to be shocked.

"It wasn't planned, and the timing is awful," she started.

"Is there ever a good time for your life to change to this degree?" He winked, and she realized she'd been holding her breath. She released the oxygen from her lungs.

"I guess not. But I just started this job—"

"These things happen, Courtney. It's life, with all of its crazy twists and turns," he stated with compassion, and she was so grateful for his understanding.

"Looks like there's a lot I can do around here to support the team." She referred to riding a desk for the rest of her pregnancy.

"We need every deputy we have right now. The

task force can use a seasoned officer on it. You'll be just as valuable in here as you would be out there." He bit back a yawn.

"I can start by kicking you out of here so you can grab some shut-eye," she urged.

"That's probably a good idea." The bags under his eyes were no joke.

"Where are we with Gus?" she asked.

"He'll be transported in another couple of hours. He's on suicide watch. They're making arrangements for him at Cedars Bay," an inpatient facility that had a special wing for housing suspects and the criminally insane. Zach rubbed the scruff on his chin.

"I'm guessing he didn't give us anything to work with on Breanna's case." It was worth mentioning, but she got her expected answer in the form of a head shake. "What does your gut tell you about Gus?"

"He has an enormous amount of guilt over something that he did, which says he's done something that he's not proud of. What is it? I have no idea. Do I think he's our guy? I can't be certain one way or the other. He's an emotional mess, but that could be because of his actions, in which case he's not likely to repeat the crime. He could have slowly unraveled since then." Zach bit back a yawn. "Pardon me."

"Thanks for the update. I shouldn't keep you awake," she said. "I'm sorry about my problem."

He locked gazes with her, and his expression morphed to concern. "You're going to be okay with all this, right?"

She knew he was talking about the pregnancy. "I will be in time. I mean, I *can* get there, but I'm not there yet. You know what I mean?"

"I think I do." Zach was a good friend and a great boss.

"Mind if we keep the reason I'm on desk duty between us until I get the all clear from my doctor in a few weeks?" She hoped that wouldn't be an issue.

"You say what you want when you're ready. No one will hear a word from me," he promised, and she believed him. Zach's word was as good it came.

"Thanks, Zach. You can't know how much I appreciate that." His expression said he could come close.

"People do have a way of figuring these things out no matter how quiet we're being." He was right about that. People would talk. It was normal for folks to care what happened in each other's lives in Jacobstown.

"I won't be able to hide it forever," she said with a small smile. "Right now, I'm ready to focus on my job."

"Let me get you set up with a volunteer." He stood and ushered her through the door and to the hallway. "I have an office set up next door to mine occupied by someone I trust with my life. It's Jordan, so if you'd rather now work with him this would be a good time to mention it."

"I promise I have enough on my mind right now not to worry about working with him." She stopped next to the closed door, stepping aside to let Zach take the lead. He tapped on it a couple of times before opening it.

"Jordan, you'll be working closely with Courtney," Zach said.

Courtney's body stiffened, but she forced her shoulders to relax and her heart rate to calm down from its frantic rhythm. As it was, her heart pounded her chest like an out-of-control hammer.

Jordan glanced up from the notebook he'd been studying in time to acknowledge her with a nod. He stood up out of respect. "Come on in. We can use all the help we can get."

Normally, Zach would pick up on the undertone in his cousin's voice, but he didn't seem to this time. It was probably due to lack of sleep. Nothing usually got past the man.

"I'll be in my office with the lights out for about the next hour if anyone needs me." Zach paused a beat as his gaze shifted from Courtney to Jordan. "You two will be okay, right?"

"Of course." Courtney shooed him away. "No one's waking you up if I have anything to say about it. We can handle things around here while you catch a nap."

Zach saluted before returning to his office next door, as promised.

"I'm going to get a cup of coffee," Jordan said before shutting his notebook on the table in front of him. "You want anything from the break room?"

"No, thanks."

Courtney wished she would've asked him to brief her on what he was working on before he disappeared down the hall. She also didn't want to think about how badly she wanted a cup of coffee right then and how sick it would make her if she gave in to the craving. She wished she could have decaf, but the smell wafting down the hall from the break room was making her sick. The only time she didn't get sick around coffee was when she'd kissed Jordan. His breath had the taste of it mixed with peppermint. The kiss stirred a few other senses that she didn't need to think about.

She walked over to the round table. The space had been set up like a war room. A map of the Kent ranch and surrounding ranches was pinned on a corkboard. There were blue stick pins dotting the landscape, most of them along Rushing Creek. This must be what Jordan was working on.

He seemed to be tagging all the places animals had been found. There were yellow stick pins, too. She figured the different colors represented the kind of animal found there. And then there was a lone white stick pin at the location where Breanna had been found. Courtney's heart squeezed thinking about the tragedy.

Jordan strolled into the room, looking a little too good in his jeans and button-down shirt. She realized he had on the same shirt as last night, too. Had he been here all night?

She glanced behind him to make sure no one followed him. "I'm on desk duty, and I told him about us. I know he's your family, but it slipped out. I'm sorry I didn't give you the chance to tell him yourself."

"It's not a problem, Courtney. I thought my name might come up." His low rumble of a voice was even sexier without sleep. She remembered how good it had been at seducing her. She could listen to that man talk all day and never get tired of hearing his voice. This wasn't the time to let herself get carried away by Jordan Kent or how good he sounded. "How'd he take the news?"

"He was good about it," she said. "We're keeping it under wraps around here until I get the green light from my doctor. I'm sure word will spread once you start sharing the news."

"No one I plan to tell will breathe a word of

this until I give the okay," he quickly countered. There was an edge to his voice now, and she'd be damned if he didn't sound even sexier.

"I'm on desk duty, and I've been paired up with you. Fill me in on what all this is about." She folded her arms and hugged her elbows to her chest.

"It's probably obvious what's going on here." He pointed to the map.

She nodded. "I meant to ask Zach if we got anything back from forensics on the contents of the freezer bag."

"The DNA matched Breanna's." He stood in respectful silence for a long moment.

It was probably just the news turning Courtney's stomach, but she ran to the nearest garbage can and emptied what little was in there. It was strange that crime felt so much more personal in Jacobstown. In a big department like Dallas, violent crimes rarely ever hit so close to home. Maybe that was the reason the massacre a year ago hurt so badly. It had felt so personal.

More heaves racked her.

Jordan was beside her before she could tell him to stay away. His hand was on her back, making small circles, reassuring her that she'd be okay.

When she finally stopped heaving, she thanked him and then excused herself to the bathroom. In her purse, she'd tucked a toothbrush and tooth-paste. She pulled them out and brushed her teeth.

And then she took a long, hard look at herself. Her identity had been tied to being in law enforcement. What if she couldn't hack the job anymore? What was she in a different job? She'd allowed her work to consume her for the past decade. She'd even dated another cop, one who would always keep an emotional distance.

The revelation almost knocked her back a step. Decks had never comforted her when she was upset. In fact, when she'd gotten emotional during their relationship, she'd go into the bathroom to cry. Had she ever let him see the real her? The short answer to that question was a fast *no*. Dating someone in law enforcement gave a sense of comradery but not intimacy. The connection they felt was stronger than buddies but short of love.

Courtney knew on instinct her relationship with Jordan had been different. It had scared the hell out of her. And she'd done the thing she did best—pushed him out of her life.

She pulled out her cell phone and stared at the picture she'd taken of the counselor's business card. Her finger hovered over the name. Why was taking that first step so hard? She'd called dozens of new numbers every month. Why did looking at this one and thinking about pulling the trigger make it suddenly hard to breathe?

After tucking her phone in her purse, she splashed cold water on her face. The call could wait.

TEN HOURS OF staring at a map, talking theories and overseeing volunteers had Courtney needing fresh air. Her nausea had subsided hours ago, and she'd been able to get a decent meal down for lunch. It had held her until the last hour, when her stomach decided to remind her she hadn't eaten in a while. The little nugget was demanding.

She stood up and then rolled her neck around to ease the tension in her muscles.

"I'll be back in a little while," she said to Jordan.

"Are you going out to grab something to eat?" He didn't look up.

"Yes."

"You want company?" he asked.

"No, thanks. I have plans." She didn't see the need to tell him that she was dining with her neighbor. Most everything about her life was about to become public knowledge—or so it felt—so she'd hold on to what little privacy she had left.

"With who?" Jordan glanced up. A mix of emotion she couldn't quite pinpoint darkened his gaze. Jealousy? She was most likely seeing what she wanted to. It was probably normal for her to want the father of her child to be a little bit jealous even though she was eating with an almost seventy-five-year-old widow. He didn't know that, and she hadn't expected any reaction from him at all.

"Just a friend," she said quietly. Defensively?

She wasn't trying to hurt his feelings.

He mumbled something about just trying to make sure she didn't have to eat alone and refocused on the map he'd been studying.

Courtney didn't want to be late to supper with Mrs. Farmer. She'd instantly liked her neighbor, and after last night Courtney felt a special bond with Sassy, too. A special connection was forged when put in a life-or-death situation. It was the same reason cops were so close to each other. They did life or death together every workday.

It had long since gotten dark by the time Courtney made it to her car. The winds had picked up, but the forecast called for low fifties tonight, warmer than it had been in days. That was the thing about Texas weather—even when it got freezing cold, it didn't stay that way for long.

She braced against the frigid winds, which whipped her hair around. She climbed into the driver's seat and started the engine, flipped on her headlights, and navigated out of the parking lot.

The road leading to her house was quiet. There was hardly ever any traffic, and tonight was no exception. She wound along the country road, keeping her eyes focused and alert out the front windshield. An irrational part of her brain searched for the coyote. She half expected the wild animal to run from out of the brush and explode onto her car.

The field she'd found Sassy in last night ran along one side of the road for miles. The area led to the back of the Kent property. Memories crashed down around her, and her eyes suddenly got very leaky.

Courtney didn't normally do emotional. She could blame it on last year's massacre or her current hormone levels, but suddenly she'd figured out how to cry faster than she could snap her fingers. She'd become a leaky faucet.

At the bend in the twisty road, she caught sight of a pickup parked off the road. Car trouble in this weather was no treat. Her headlights skimmed left, right and back again, moving back and forth as she wound around the road.

A moment of panic struck when she realized the pickup looked familiar. Blue Trunks? With that thought, she slowed her car and dimmed her headlights. There were no streetlamps on this stretch, so she had to leave her fog lights on or risk running off the road.

The driver of the pickup may have already seen her. She slowed to a near crawl as she approached the abandoned-looking pickup. There was no sign of anyone around, and an eerie feeling crept over her. This vehicle certainly hadn't been there this morning when Courtney drove this route to work.

She passed by a couple of times, not wanting to raise the alarm for a pickup that she wasn't exactly certain belonged to a guy she'd seen favoring his left foot at The Mart yesterday. Besides, it didn't look like anyone was inside.

Courtney made a U-turn and cruised by the pickup, repeating the path a couple of times to make certain there would be no surprises. She rolled her window down as she pulled beside the vehicle.

She shone her flashlight into the cab and saw a cell phone on the bench seat. If someone was stranded, wouldn't they take their cell with them? This area got service. Sure, it could be patchy, but they had it in several places.

Courtney picked up her radio to call in a suspicious vehicle when she heard an ear-piercing shriek coming from the wooded area beyond the field. Her pulse kicked up a few notches as she relayed her location to dispatch.

She hopped out of her SUV and palmed her weapon as she raced toward the sound. Someone was in trouble, and a force inside her took over despite her logical mind telling her to play it slow. If she could save a life, she had no choice but to try, so she bolted toward the tree line.

All thoughts of the coyote came rushing back,

but she had no time to hesitate. If an animal had attacked someone who'd cut through the field, Courtney had to try to respond. She faintly heard that backup was on its way, and the closest deputy was twenty minutes to the east of her location.

Whoever made that scream might not have twenty minutes to live. Courtney was on autopilot as she pushed her legs to move faster, her flashlight in her left hand and her Glock in her right. She'd shoot any jerk who tried to charge toward her.

The flashlight did a great job of lighting the path in front of her, but she instantly realized that she was vulnerable to a side or rear attack once she reached the thicket, so she intentionally slowed her pace.

Another scream, muffled this time, sent a second shot of adrenaline coursing through her. She was on the right track, because the noise was closer.

Branches slapped Courtney's face, and she had to stomp through the underbrush, but she kept pushing forward. She was making headway and would come upon the scene in seconds instead of minutes at this pace.

And then a blood-curdling scream stopped Courtney in her tracks.

Chapter Thirteen

Courtney mumbled a protection prayer she'd learned as a small child and made a beeline toward the noise. On the edge of her flashlight beam, she caught sight of a male figure. He disappeared into the trees in a matter of seconds.

Training kicked in, warning her not to run straight to the victim. In all honesty, she wanted to even if that would be a rookie mistake. The area had to be secured first and foremost, or the attacker could return and dispense with them both. Courtney couldn't afford to let her guard down. But the gurgling noises coming from fifteen feet in front of her nearly stopped her heart.

Using her flashlight, she skimmed the ground, stopping on the victim. There was blood everywhere and more pumping out of her every second. Courtney had to fight against all her instincts to render aid.

If she made a wrong move, they'd both be dead

and she'd be no use to the victim, Courtney reminded herself. This was the part of the job she had a hard time stomaching. Seeing someone hurt—dying?—and not being able to run to them was the worst feeling. A flashback to the massacre, the blood that ran down the street and into the gutter, assaulted her. The blank look in Decks's eyes when she finally got to him. She'd been shot, too, but spared death. It seemed unfair to her that she should live when everyone on her team and her boyfriend didn't.

"Help is here, so I need you to hang on," she tried to soothe the victim, knowing that her words were empty. She couldn't help, not yet, not in the way she wanted to.

A noise like a dying animal echoed, causing Courtney's heart to clench. She scanned the area for the male figure as she moved around the perimeter, but there was no sign of him.

Courtney listened for any indication he was still around or any other opportunistic creature that might be lurking in the shadows waiting to get the drop on her. When she heard none and confirmed by sight there wasn't anyone or anything around, she radioed for help.

Then, and only then, did she let herself run to the victim.

The blonde woman was splayed on the ground, her arms and legs spread out at odd angles. Courtney dropped to her knees beside her. There was blood everywhere and Courtney didn't recognize the victim. She couldn't be more than twenty-five years old. But where was all that blood coming from?

"Stay with me, sweetie," Courtney said.

The blonde tried to talk but couldn't.

"Nod your head if you knew the person who did this to you," Courtney said. The tacky smell of blood filled the air as it gushed from the side of her head.

No response came.

The woman gasped for air as she shivered, and her gaze fixed on Courtney's face.

"No. No. No. No." There was no clear passageway in order to perform CPR. Blood gushed from the victim's nose and mouth. There was nothing Courtney could do besides feel helpless and like she'd just failed in the worst way.

Where was all the blood coming from? Courtney couldn't pinpoint all the locations. She used her flashlight to scan the victim's body and saw gashes everywhere in the back and sides of her head. She bit back a curse.

"Please stay with me," Courtney said as a few tears leaked. Not again. Courtney's heart squeezed so hard she thought it might burst. This person was too young to die.

She heard static on the radio before Lopez's voice came through.

"Where are you?" she asked Lopez.

"I don't see a pickup truck, but I do see your vehicle," Lopez said.

"I'm east about ten minutes into the woods. I need an ambulance." She was doing her best to keep it together no matter how much she wanted to break down. Looking at the victim, Courtney made a vow to nail the jerk who did this.

Courtney's next clear thought was that she wanted to see Jordan. There was something comforting about his presence. She told herself it was because she was carrying his child and he was in full-on protective daddy mode. But there was more to it than she was willing to admit.

Within minutes, the scene was flooded with personnel. Queasiness took over, and she had to step away.

In the light, Courtney recognized the blonde. Her name was Rhonda Keller, and she'd been a couple of grades below Courtney in school. Rhonda had dyed her hair blond.

"Is that the Kellers' daughter?" Deputy Lopez asked.

"Yes," Courtney confirmed. "Where's Zach?"

"He was signing paperwork on Gus," Lopez informed. "Said he'd be here as soon as he could get away."

Courtney recounted the story of what happened.

She realized that she'd forgotten all about dinner with Mrs. Farmer. "Will you write this up? I need to make a call."

Lopez nodded. "Of course. Let me know if there's anything else I can do. Take a break. You look like you need a minute."

"Lingering stomach issues" was all she said. She stepped out of earshot and called Mrs. Farmer.

"Hello." Mrs. Farmer sounded worried.

"It's me. Courtney."

"Oh, I don't have on my reading glasses, and those little screens are impossible to make out," Mrs. Farmer said.

"I'm sorry about dinner. I ended up on a work call," Courtney explained.

"That's all right, dear." It made everything worse that Mrs. Farmer made an effort to cover the disappointment in her voice. "I hope you caught him."

"No. He got away," Courtney admitted. "You'll hear about this soon enough on the news, but a woman was assaulted near our homes. He got away, so I want you to be extra careful. Stay inside tonight, okay?"

"That's terrible news, Courtney. I'm so sorry." Those last three words threatened to break her down.

Instead of giving in to the wave of emotion

building, Courtney thanked Mrs. Farmer and then got off the phone. She stared down at her cell for a long time, wishing she could bring something besides disappointment to people.

She had a moment. The kind when she knew someone was making a beeline for her and not trying to hide the fact. She glanced up...and there he came. Jordan Kent stalked toward her. She expected to see frustration on his face but saw only compassion. So she moved toward it, toward him. And the next thing she knew she was being hauled against his chest as she threw her arms around his neck, buried her face and cried.

Courtney had no idea when Zach arrived at the scene. It didn't matter. She held on to Jordan like he was the only lifeboat in the middle of a raging storm.

"I got the picture of the pickup you sent," Zach said to her, and she faintly registered the sound of his voice in the background. "I'm putting it out with every law enforcement official in the area and with the volunteers. Let's get some heat on this guy and make it impossible for him to show his face or stay on the road."

Courtney took a step back to address her boss. "Yes, sir."

"Maybe someone will recognize it and turn him in," Jordan's calming voice said.

"Cases have been solved on less. We're putting out the picture with a tip line." There was a pause before he focused on Courtney. "What do you think about doing back to the ranch with Jordan? I'll stop by to talk to you later. You did a great job tonight."

Courtney didn't agree. A victim had died in Courtney's arms.

"The ranch sounds good." She needed a minute to regroup anyway. The thought of going home alone sat hard on her chest. Before Courtney could put up an argument, she was being led out of the trees and away from the field. She didn't have the energy to argue. The fight had drained from her.

Jordan deposited her in his vehicle.

"My car," she started to protest.

"You have the keys?" he asked.

She pulled them off the clip on her belt and handed them over.

"I'll have someone pick it up and bring it to the ranch. Is there anything you need from it while we're here?" He took a step back, and panic engulfed her.

She grabbed on to his arm. "Don't disappear on me. Please."

She didn't know where that had come from, but the feeling in her chest that if he walked away she'd never see him again was real.

"Okay." He seemed to be trying to assess her mental fitness.

"I know that I'm acting irrationally. But, please, don't leave me alone right now." He glanced down at her arm, and it was clear to both of them that she was trembling.

"I'm not going anywhere but here." He clicked the lock button on her key. "I won't leave your sight. Okay?"

She leaned back in the passenger seat and clicked on her seat belt while nodding.

He climbed into the cab of the truck and managed to slip over her, which was a feat considering his brawn and height.

Once he settled into the driver's seat, he touched her hand. "You're safe, Courtney."

"She's dead, Jordan. I couldn't save her."

"I know. There was nothing you could do, Courtney. It wasn't your fault," he said.

So, why did it feel like it?

JORDAN HANDED COURTNEY a second cup of chamomile. She'd showered in the guest bathroom and put on borrowed clothes from Jordan's sister-in-law Leah, who was close to the same size. Deacon and Leah lived on the property, like the other siblings, along with their son, Carter.

"You haven't eaten dinner yet, and it's late," he said to Courtney as she took the mug from him. She was curled up on the couch in the family room and looked a little too right being in his family home. He'd poured himself a cup of coffee and was half-done by the time she spoke.

"I don't think I could keep anything down." She'd sat in that spot and stared at the same wall for the past twenty minutes.

"What about the soup? And maybe some crackers?" he urged for lack of a better idea. Feeding someone was something he figured his mother would have tried to do in this situation, and his mother was usually right about these things.

"I could try." There was no emotion in those words, and he figured she was solely trying to appease him. If it kept her healthy and strong, he'd take it.

He moved into the kitchen and heated a bowl. He found a tray and set the warmed soup on it along with a handful of salty crackers. After arranging the items on the tray, he returned to the family room. He set the tray down next to her.

"Or we could eat at the table if you'd like it better," he said.

"You don't have to fuss over me, Jordan. I'll be all right in a minute." Again, there was no conviction in her words.

"You can be whatever you need to be, Courtney. I've known you a helluva long time. I know how much of a fighter you are, so I know you won't let this win. But I also know that closing up and not talking about something only makes it fester. I'm here. I'm not going anywhere. I know you—"

She put her hand up to stop him from finishing.

"No. You need to hear this. You're one of the strongest people I know. I admire your courage. But you don't have to go it alone. No one has to be that strong," he said.

"Easy for you to say, Jordan. You're literally the toughest person I've ever met. You have a family to lean on who supports each other and genuinely cares. I've had myself to depend on. I'm good at being alone." She didn't look him in the eye. Instead, she rolled the edge of the pillow in between her thumb and forefinger. "I don't know how to let anyone else in. I don't lean on other people because they'll only let you down or leave you. Maybe not at first, but at some point, they leave. I'm not going through it again. I don't care who it's with or how long I've known them. You think I'm strong. In reality, I'm not built for that kind of disappointment."

Her words were knife stabs straight through the middle of his chest. He knew better than to take them to heart. Since her mind seemed made up, he decided not to push it. She was overwrought with emotion. Still, she wasn't alone and needed to know it.

"You may not think I'm going to be there for you, and I'm not going to try to convince you otherwise. But I need you to know that I won't walk away from my child. That baby growing in you binds us, like it or not. I have every intention of being there for him or her," he stated.

She didn't argue, and he could see by her body language that she was slowly letting go of the anger she'd felt moments ago. It would be easy to defend himself to her, but she needed proof that he would be there. Words amounted to little more than empty promises to her. He could understand that when he thought about her upbringing and then what had happened last year.

Actions spoke the loudest. It would take time.

He slowly sipped his coffee in silence. Jordan was patient. Patience won battles, and this was one war he couldn't afford to lose, no matter how much her words wounded him. They were only words. Actions were better indicators of what someone was thinking. Hers had been to cling to him in her moment of distress.

A knock at the door interrupted them.

Jordan excused himself and made the trek through the kitchen and down the hallway. This home was built before open-concept living was popular. The ceilings were high and the rooms large. It had a nice flow with the main room in the front hallway, which led to the kitchen.

Zach opened the door before Jordan could get there. His cousin had a key and was used to letting himself in. He'd practically grown up at the ranch along with his sister, Amy.

"How is she?" Zach asked before Jordan could greet his cousin.

Jordan twisted his face and lowered his voice. "Not good."

"I can't believe I didn't see the signs before now," Zach started in. "She's showing symptoms of post-traumatic stress disorder, and I have to assume it's connected to what she experienced in Dallas. The department declared her mentally competent in her file, so I didn't question it."

"She's too smart for them. They didn't know." Jordan took a moment to let Zach's revelation sink in. "She has nightmares."

"Oh."

"I know she told you that I'm the father." There was no sense dancing around the topic.

"Congratulations." Zach pulled Jordan into a brotherly hug.

"Thanks, cousin. I'm still trying to wrap my mind around being a father, but none of that will matter if she's not okay." There. He'd said it. He didn't even realize that's what was eating away at him until just now.

"I understand. Let's take care of her as much as she wants us to," Zach said.

"How are we supposed to do that? Because I seem to be making it worse." Jordan didn't like saying those words, even though they were true. He feared he was making everything harder than it needed to be, saying all the wrong things.

"We'll figure it out," Zach reassured. "In the meantime, I have news about what happened tonight."

This was the first conversation he'd had about having a baby to someone other than Courtney, and he appreciated the support from Zach. "Let's go talk to her."

Chapter Fourteen

Jordan led Zach into the family room, where he was surprised to see that Courtney had finished off the bowl of soup and eaten more than half of the crackers. The tray was sitting on the coffee table and Kitty—it was the name given the feral cat who kept showing up for meals and eventually wormed its way inside the house—was curled up in Courtney's lap as she absently stroked its fur. Courtney glanced at him with a look of apology, which he acknowledged with a nod and half a smile.

One great thing about being around someone he had history with, someone like Courtney, was that words weren't always necessary to communicate. A look, a nod could say so much between two people who were tuned in to each other.

"What's going on, Zach?" She turned her attention to her boss, who took a seat on the chair next to the leather couch.

Jordan took a seat on the matching couch opposite Courtney.

"The initial evidence is pointing to this being a separate crime," Zach started. "Rhonda Keller was home for an extended stay after filing for divorce from her new husband. She'd been communicating with her boyfriend from high school, Hughey Brown."

"I remember him. Wasn't he the captain of the basketball team?" Courtney asked, and Jordan rocked his head.

"The two decided to meet up and party, which they did in the field. Hughey says they kissed, but as things started to get hot and heavy she 'freaked out' and started hitting him for breaking up with her in high school to go out with Susan Wells," Zach continued.

This was like a blast from the past. Jordan remembered hearing about it during football practice when he was in school.

"The two argued, and Hughey says he decided he didn't want to repeat the same mistakes he'd made in high school, so he left. He said she might've been on something other than the tequila shots they did," Zach continued.

"So, he just left her there?" Courtney's shock was evident in her voice.

"She drove away from their meet-up spot but ended up with a flat tire." Zach rubbed the scruff on his chin. "Hughey claims he didn't know about it. He says the field is where it ended between the two of them. He told her to grow up and then took off. He says her car was there so he didn't worry about her getting home."

"What was his reaction to hearing she was murdered?" Courtney asked.

"He broke down and started crying. His demeanor changed almost immediately. He said he thought she'd filed assault charges or asked for a restraining order to get him back for leaving her again." Zach's brow arched. "But when we told him the news, he seemed genuinely shocked."

"He was a jerk in high school, and he still sounds like a jerk, though," Courtney said. "What kind of person gets drunk with someone and then leaves them to fend for themselves instead of seeing them home and especially with a killer on the loose?"

"Not anyone I want my sister or cousins to know," Zach stated.

"Everyone is on high alert right now. That was a jerk move." Courtney stroked Kitty a little faster.

"He left her vulnerable." Zach paused a beat. "But there are no witnesses to corroborate his story."

"Does that mean you think Hughey might be the killer?" Courtney's hands trembled.

"He's being detained while we decide on

whether or not we're going to file criminal charges against him. We're looking at public intoxication for one and, of course, more serious charges if that's what the evidence dictates," Zach informed. "Rhonda had a flat tire, and the pickup you saw might've stopped to render aid. If Hughey's story holds water, Rhonda might've trusted the wrong person."

"It's happened before. Ted Bundy comes to mind, but there were plenty of others. This guy might've walked with a limp or a cane. He could've disguised himself to look older and maybe even a little feeble in order to lower her defenses. She'd had a little too much to drink, so her judgment wasn't the best," Courtney speculated.

"He could've offered her a ride into town," Zach added.

"Once she's inside his vehicle, he thinks he has it made—and he probably does." Courtney worked the corner of the pillow in between her thumb and forefinger. "Except this has to be related to the Jacobstown Hacker. We'd assumed that he's an opportunistic killer based on Breanna's murder. Maybe he cruises around looking for targets."

"That's a good point. The odds of him driving up at the exact moment she needs help are slim, though," Zach pointed out.

"And the fact that Rhonda got a flat tire in the first place bugs me. I mean, it happens, but right at the moment she gets into a fight with her ex from high school? And then an opportunistic killer happens upon her?" Courtney issued a sharp breath.

"The killer could've wandered upon the fight without either of them knowing. He might've been scouting a location. That property backs up to the Kent Ranch and we all know Rushing Creek meanders nearby," Zach said.

"It's possible that's how he's been accessing the land all along," Jordan agreed. "I don't think we have any cameras on that side of the fencing."

"If he was watching the fight and realized she'd be a good mark, maybe he put a hole in her tire or created a slow leak," Courtney said.

"All of which makes sense," Zach concluded.

"And then there's the idea that Rhonda's argument got heated with Hughey and his temper flew out of control. The words turned physical and he killed her," Courtney said.

"Mike said there were multiple blows to the head with something that resembled the blade of an ax." Zach's face twisted in disgust at the coroner's finding. The thought that any human being was sick enough to do that to another person was mind-boggling.

"The killer might not have been planning on targeting anyone tonight. Maybe he came upon the scene and figured this was the time to act," Courtney offered.

"In which case he might've made his first mistake," Zach said. "We'll check her system for ketamine."

"I interrupted him. It could be the reason for the change in MO." There was so much sadness in Courtney's voice when she spoke those words aloud.

Jordan knew the guy they were looking for was calculating. This crime didn't fit the MO of the Jacobstown Hacker. He didn't normally strike the head. In fact, there was normally no evidence he'd been at a crime scene. Zach was still trying to figure out if the victims were killed ahead of time and taken to the spot where he'd cut off their foot or if the victim was drugged and carried to the spot. Someone who'd been bludgeoned in the head with an ax multiple times as opposed to one clean whack on the left ankle right above the foot didn't fit the bill. The date-rape drug ketamine had been found in Breanna's system, which could've explained why she didn't put up a fight. And Courtney made a good point about interrupting the killer.

Then there was Hughey to consider. He'd always been known for his bad temper. In high school he'd pushed a kid down the stairs for cutting him off. Being a star on the basketball team had gotten him out of suspension. The coach had smoothed things over with the dean of students.

Athletes in Texas high schools were treated too much like rock stars.

Someone angry, who'd just been in a heated argument with an ex, might whack her the minute she turned around. But why would there be an ax anywhere near them? How would that have happened, exactly? Did the two take the ax into the woods to their love nest? And where was this supposed love nest to begin with? It had to be in the field somewhere. Only an idiot went into the trees and underbrush after dark. It was cold outside, so they wouldn't be eaten by mosquitoes, but there were plenty of opportunistic animals lurking around. Animals that would no doubt pick an easy meal.

There were a lot of unanswered questions in this case that would leave the town spinning. Half the folks were out on neighborhood watches, trying to protect each other and keep each other safe. That could also explain the killer's change in MO. Maybe he was starting to act out of desperation.

"Any word on the Barstock sighting?" Courtney asked Zach.

"No one else has seen him. Just Liesel at the diner." Zach's phone started dinging.

"Any chance she confused him with someone else?" Courtney asked.

"No." Zach checked his screen and then glanced

over at Jordan. "Would you mind if I spoke to Courtney alone for a minute?"

Jordan instinctively checked with Courtney, who nodded.

"Not a problem. I'll be in the next room if you need me," Jordan said. He left the room quickly. Although he wasn't eager for the conversation to happen.

If he had to guess, Zach was telling Courtney to take leave. Not because of the pregnancy but because of what had happened earlier that night and the signs of PTSD. After what she'd seen and experienced, Zach would want a full evaluation on her mental fitness before allowing her back on the job. Being put on desk duty had been difficult. He feared this news would set her back even more.

Jordan busied himself in the kitchen.

Much to his surprise, Zach strolled in a couple of minutes later.

"Everything okay?" he asked his cousin.

"She asked for you," Zach informed. "I can see myself out."

Jordan said goodbye before excusing himself and walking into the family room. Courtney sat there, feet tucked underneath her legs, looking more at home than he'd seen her in days.

"I have to take a few days leave," she said, and she sounded resigned to the fact.

"Would it make a difference if I talked to Zach?" He wanted to do something to help.

"It's protocol, but I suspect there's more to it than that if I'm being honest." She issued a sharp breath and fixed her gaze on a spot on the wall across from her. "I can see it in his face. He's worried about me."

Jordan took a seat next to her. "I'm sorry."

"He's right. I've been trying to convince myself that I'm fine, but I'm not and the truth just keeps stalking me," she said. "It's not going away unless I face it head-on. That's been made painfully clear to me."

"Is this about what happened last year?" He didn't want to push her, but he knew she hadn't honestly spoken about the incident in Dallas with anyone.

"What do you know about it?" She didn't look at him, and that was good. His heart went out to her for everything she'd been through, and he had a feeling her pain might be present in her eyes.

"Only what was in the news," he admitted. This was the time she normally shut down on him and quit talking. Usually he could almost feel the walls going up between them. She'd been through even more tonight, and he saw her strength and bravery. But how much more could one person take? Bottle everything up, shake the bottle and eventually the cap would come shooting off in a massive explosion. Zach could handle the stress that came with the job because he didn't bottle up his emotions.

Zach also had an amazing support network. He talked about what bothered him, and Jordan knew his cousin encouraged his deputies to take good care of themselves.

Looking at Courtney and not seeing her as fragile but someone who was trying to be too strong, Jordan couldn't help wondering whom she had to lean on. She'd been honest about that earlier.

"Eight officers killed that day in Dallas were friends or associates of mine. One of them, Decks, was my boyfriend." The words, spoken slow and deliberate, reminded him of the way she used to talk in high school when she was holding in emotion. "One of the officers killed, the one who was my boyfriend, had a nine-year-old son, Joey."

Jordan didn't want to hear about Courtney's love life, but he had no claim on her and no right to be jealous.

"Were you close with Joey?" As a girlfriend and not a spouse, Courtney would have no legal right to visit the child.

"No." She shrugged. "I've never even met him."

Jordan couldn't say he understood. His brow must've shot up because she went on to explain.

"A pension isn't enough to bring up a child, let alone send him to college if he wants to go, so I give half of my salary to his mother through a blind trust fund that I set up. She doesn't deserve to have to bring her child up alone with almost no support." Courtney paused a beat. "Now that I'm pregnant, I have another little one to think about."

"If you're worried about money, don't. I can help with anything you need," he said quickly.

"I have to pay my own way through life, Jordan." Her tone left no room for argument, so he figured he'd shelve the conversation for now. There'd be plenty of time to figure out finances, and he hadn't meant to offend her.

"I keep asking one question. Why me? Why am I still alive?" It wasn't like Courtney to feel sorry for herself, and he didn't think she was looking for an answer from him, so he waited for her to finish. "Why did I get to live and not them?"

Those words spoken aloud seemed to carry the weight of the world.

"I don't know, Courtney. But I, for one, am grateful you're here," he said.

She turned to him, climbed on his lap and kissed him.

COURTNEY KNEW THIS was dangerous territory, but she couldn't care about that right now. Kissing Jordan seemed like the most natural thing to do under the circumstances. She couldn't deny that she'd missed him over the last six weeks. She had.

She expected him to pull back and set her straight again. He didn't.

Instead he looped his arms around her waist and crushed her against his muscled chest.

His tongue in her mouth, his hands roaming her back sent electric impulses flaring through her body, warming places where his fingers trailed. His hands were big, and it felt like one could cover half her back.

She tunneled her fingers in his thick hair and deepened the kiss—a kiss she'd wanted to repeat ever since the other night.

Courtney couldn't help it. Her pull to him was the strongest she'd ever felt with anyone. She'd tried to convince herself that it was shared history, but there was so much more to it than that. It's also what scared the hell out of her. This wasn't the time to get inside her head. This was the time to feel her way through her next steps.

And the most logical next step that came to mind was to really feel Jordan, to feel his bare, naked skin against hers. To feel his weight on top of her pushing her into the mattress. To feel his hands roam all over her body.

No one had ever made her feel sexier or more alive and in the moment than Jordan.

Courtney's hands flew to the buttons on his shirt on autopilot. Her fingers trembled with need, so she fumbled a little bit.

There was a moment of hesitation on his part, and she feared this was the point when he'd stop her. But Jordan covered her hands with his, paused for a beat and then helped her finish.

A few seconds later, he shrugged out of his shirt while their lips pressed together.

Courtney wanted this more than anything. Still, a nagging question tugged at the back of her mind.

Was this a mistake?

Chapter Fifteen

Courtney pulled back long enough to look into Jordan's eyes. She needed reassurance that what was happening between them was okay.

Jordan pressed his forehead to hers and closed his eyes.

"I want this to happen, Jordan."

"So do I. More than you could know. But we're making progress, and I need to know this won't confuse the issue." He was being smart. She couldn't deny it.

"I've held someone who died in my arms earlier tonight, Jordan. I've lost people that I cared about in a snap. We can think about tomorrow and the next day and the next after that, but no one knows for certain if we'll be there to make all our plans happen. All we really have is right here, right now. And all I know is that I've missed this." There. She'd said it. "I don't know what that means or how much that complicates our lives, but I want you right now, Jordan. And I need to know you want this, too."

He opened his eyes—golden-brown eyes that had darkened with need.

For a long moment, he just stared at her like he was looking right through her. And he probably was. She couldn't care about that right now. She'd opened up to him earlier. She actually liked talking to him, and it felt like part of the weight that had been sucking her under for far too long was lifting. It would take time and understanding before she could even think about healing, but for the first time in her life, she could see a peek of light in a world that had been dark for too long.

She wanted to run toward it but knew that was asking too much of herself all at once. But she could take baby steps.

"You're sure this is what you want?" His voice was low and sexy. That deep timbre washed over her and through her.

"I've never been more certain of anything in my life." It was true. With all the craziness that she'd experienced over her lifetime, she was right where she wanted to be in this moment. She needed to block out the world, if only for a little while, and remember that she was still alive even if she wasn't living fully.

The realization struck a chord with her.

"And this won't make things more confusing between us," he said.

"I can't promise that." A smirk toyed with the corners of her mouth. She should probably just lie and say that it wouldn't. Courtney couldn't be dishonest with Jordan. He deserved the truth.

"What?" There was a hint of defensiveness in his tone.

"How much worse can it make it?"

His answer came in the form of covering her mouth with his in the kind of kiss that would make her knees rubbery if she was standing. She'd have to grip the wall behind her or risk falling flat on her back.

It was Jordan's turn to unbutton her shirt. His fingers worked their magic as her nipples beaded, straining for his touch. The guttural groan he released when her shirt hit the floor and he traced her lacy bra with his fingertips made warmth pool between her thighs.

She couldn't be sure if it was because he was so hot standing there or that she hadn't had sex with Jordan for six weeks, but her stomach literally quivered at his lightest touch. Whatever they had was so much more than shared history or hot sex. Was it love?

Courtney couldn't go there with anyone, but this was the closest she could imagine being to it.

Jordan's erection throbbed against her heat. A

layer of denim and a pair of cotton shorts amounted to too much material between them. With a flick, Jordan undid the snap of her bra. He was a little too skilled at that little move, but this wasn't the time to think about that. And then he cupped her full breasts in his palms as his lips crushed down on hers and her bra tumbled to the floor.

Everything disappeared except the two of them in this moment. Everything except the need pulsing through her and the tide of desire stirring, rising from deep within. Everything felt right in the world for just a moment.

Courtney dug her knees into the couch cushion and pushed herself up as she threaded her fingers through his thick mane and kissed him back, hard.

"We need to finish this in the other room so we're not interrupted." Jordan picked her up like she weighed nothing and she was reminded he'd taken her to the main house and not his place.

For a split second, she panicked about the thought of someone walking in on them or finding her there in the main house in their current condition. The notion was fleeting. What did she care? Her pregnancy was about to be revealed, and everyone would know who the father was soon enough. Would it really shock anyone that the two of them had slept together?

Inside Jordan's bedroom, he set her down on the edge of the bed. His jeans and boxers hit the floor a few seconds later, and she made quick work of letting her shorts and panties join them. It was a little too late for a condom—not like she trusted those things anymore—so neither bothered discussing using one this time. Lot of good those conversations had done during their week of hot sex.

The miniblinds let just enough moonlight into the room for her to see Jordan clearly. His body was muscled perfection. His thick, straining erection was silky skin over steel. "You'll laugh at me for saying this, Jordan. But you're beautiful."

True enough, a laugh rumbled out of his chest. "I'm not," he countered. "But you are."

"You don't have to—"

"Yes. I do. You're incredible, Courtney. I'm not just talking about your looks. You have those in spades. Your sense of humor. The way you laugh. I'd be lying if I said I didn't miss you," he admitted.

She took his hands in hers and tugged him toward her. She settled on the bed, and he positioned himself in the V of her thighs. Looking into his eyes, she guided his tip inside her. He put most of his weight on his arms as he eased himself deeper.

Courtney bucked her hips as he lowered himself on top of her. His lips met hers, and she surrendered completely to everything that was happening between them. They connected physically and emotionally—in every way that counted. Who got that?

The intensity of the emotions that had happened between them had caught her off guard, and she'd balked. None of that was important now. All that mattered was this moment.

Her body was alive with impulse as she and Jordan drove faster, harder, rocketing toward the release only he could give her.

Faster. Harder. She dug her fingers into his shoulders.

He rolled her nipples in between his thumb and forefinger, causing her to shoot over the edge. Her body was a battlefield of intense electricity. All she could do was surrender to the tide and try to hang on as she catapulted toward the edge.

Just as she felt herself hit the point of no return, all his muscles tensed, and he said her name in her ear and something that sounded a lot like *I love you.*

Those three words normally gave Courtney hives, but she actually liked the sound of them coming from Jordan.

She bucked harder and reached deeper inside as she rocketed over the edge. Sensual electricity exploded inside her body as they moved in perfect rhythm.

When her body was drained of everything left inside and she tried to catch her breath, he looked at her.

"This changes things for me. I hope it does for you." He locked gazes with her. "We don't have to discuss it now, but we will when the time's right."

"I missed you, Jordan. That's all I know right now. All I care to know."

"That's enough for today." He said it so low she almost didn't hear.

Jordan rolled onto his side before pulling her in close to his body. His warm skin against hers was the best feeling. She settled into the crook of his arm and fell into a deep sleep.

JORDAN WOKE THE next morning with the sun peeking through the blinds. He glanced at the clock, which read 6:23. Days on the ranch normally started at 4:00 a.m. He'd slept in, which was uncharacteristic for him.

Waking up to Courtney lying next to him again filled his heart in ways he couldn't afford. She'd needed comfort last night. He'd been there for her. Having sex, knowing she was going to be the mother of his child, changed their relationship.

He didn't have his mind around what that meant or what he had to offer her. His life was in Idaho, running the family business there. When he'd left Jacobstown as a young man, he'd assumed it would be for good, save for holidays and special occasions.

Every time he'd visited, he felt like an outsider.

And now? It was different. Granted, he was going to have a baby now. But that was the reason this place felt more like home than he'd ever remembered. What had changed inside him?

An annoying little voice in his head seemed determined to point out that Courtney had come home. But she had her own demons at work, and aside from a rare moment here and there, she was lost inside herself.

Plus, there was the simple fact that he couldn't be in a relationship with someone who would never trust him. Jordan had been spoiled. He'd seen the kind of relationship his parents had had. The bar was set high. He could admit that. But he wouldn't settle for anything less because he'd seen the best. He'd lived the kind of love that was unconditional and grew over time to be something even more beautiful.

Something unattainable?

Being with someone who loved him with their whole heart and vice versa was the only true comfort in life. Anything less would be settling, and he'd seen how that had worked out for a few of his friends.

Jordan could admit to missing Courtney after the week at the cabin. He'd tried to discuss a serious matter with her, and she'd balked. Then she'd walked out the door and hadn't looked back. If she hit the road when things got tough once, she'd do it again. Past behavior was always the best predictor of the future. People rarely changed.

A small piece of his heart wanted to protest the logical side to him. His heart wanted to believe that she could handle a real relationship. But she'd already burned him once, and he'd never been the type to ask for a second round of punishment.

Jordan slipped out of the covers and found a fresh pair of boxers and jeans. He put on his clothes and headed toward the kitchen to make something to eat and get his caffeine fix.

He scrambled up a couple of eggs and toasted a couple slices of bread. As he ate at the granite counter, he checked his phone. The battery had died. He plugged it into the charger, and it took a few seconds to get enough juice to turn on.

By the time he'd finished his meal and drained a cup of black coffee, his cell started vibrating with messages.

Lone Star Lonnie had gone in to volunteer at Zach's office, so Jordan could take the morning to catch up on ranch affairs. Thankfully, there were no calves due for another week or two. But he needed to check on the pregnant heifers.

There were also documents he needed to sign, so he moved into the office. A stack of papers stared at him from on top of the desk. This had been his father's office. To this day, being in here was strange ever since his father had passed away.

It had been years now, and yet Jordan couldn't seem. Hell, his siblings had all found their soul mates and settled down. He'd always been the odd man out, and it seemed he would remain that way. He thought about Courtney's pregnancy, about the little nugget growing inside her. He expected to feel a sense of dread for this being unplanned. Instead, he felt a twinge of something that felt an awful lot like excitement at the thought of having his own child.

Granted, an unplanned pregnancy wasn't the way he thought he'd usher in fatherhood. In his mind, he would've followed a more traditional route of marriage and honeymoon before baby. In theory, anyway. In practice, he hadn't really thought he would find the right person or have children. Jordan loved his work. He loved being out on the land. And he loved his freedom.

Having amazing sex with the right woman was about as far as he'd ever gone with a woman. Emotional attachments got messy. He searched his thoughts for the last time he'd let himself fall for someone. His mind snapped to his high school girlfriend Sophie. He'd been head over heels for her before she got sick. The terminal brain cancer diagnosis had caught everyone off guard, including him. For years, he thought he'd cursed her in some way. Teenagers always found a way to blame themselves for every tragedy.

Damn. Had Sophie truly been the last person he'd opened up to? The only one he'd let himself love?

That annoying voice said he loved Courtney. But there was no way. She pushed him away more than she opened up to him. She most definitely didn't need that kind of upheaval in her life right now. What would loving her matter?

Jordan wouldn't risk his heart for someone who couldn't love him. Good communication and a few rounds of the best sex he'd ever had might be the most he could expect from Courtney. Would it be enough? Would she be able to stick it through with their child when times got tough? And no matter what amount of privilege a person grew up with, no one was spared losing a loved one at some point.

His phone buzzed in the kitchen, so Jordan forced himself out of his thoughts and went to answer it. Zach's name popped up. He answered the call before it rolled into voice mail. "What's up, Zach?"

"I thought you should hear this first and from me," Zach started.

That didn't sound good. "Okay."

"There's a theory circulating around town that Courtney interrupted the killer and that's why he hacked Rhonda in the back of the head in order to kill her." Zach got quiet for a long moment. He seemed to understand what that would do to her if she heard the news firsthand.

"She said as much last night. Hearing it from others won't be good for her," Jordan said.

"No, it won't." Zach issued a sharp breath.

"Is there any merit to it?" Jordan needed to know what he was dealing with before he spoke to Courtney.

"It's not an unreasonable theory." So, it might be true was what Zach was saying.

"You mentioned PTSD last night. She also has survivor's guilt," Jordan said. "She's planning to talk to a counselor about that and a few other things."

"You already know I'll support her in any way that I can." Zach was more than a good cousin. He was truly a good man.

"Thank you." Jordan meant it.

"We have to look out for our own. It's nothing any of you wouldn't do for me." Zach was right about that. Being in Idaho away from the family, Jordan was beginning to see how lonely his life had been there. He was beginning to see that it was nice to be around people who had his back and looked out for each other. All those things had felt suffocating before. What had changed in him to make him feel differently? *Fatherhood?*

He couldn't deny that he felt a pull toward being around family for his unborn nugget. The thought of him or her growing up surrounded by love wasn't the worst thing he could think of. And, besides, he was most likely going to need a ton of parenting advice. From what he could tell so far with his nieces and nephews, those kids didn't come with any sort of training manual. Once a kid came into the world, it was go time.

"Your relationships are none of my business," Zach started.

"I care what you think, even if I don't always listen to your advice, Zach."

"I appreciate that, Jordan." Zach paused a few beats. "It was bad for her growing up here with her father."

"Yes, it was. I hate that she went through all the abuse." He was already gone by that time, and his family had never been ones for gossip. So much about what Courtney had said about only being able to count on herself made even more sense as he was reminded of her traumatic upbringing. Jordan understood just how fully she meant those words, and his heart squeezed at thinking about the abuse she'd suffered.

Instead of feeling sorry for herself, she'd gone on to work in law enforcement in order to bring justice to bastards who took advantage of or hurt others. So many things snapped in place in his mind. He wanted to do everything he could to protect her from the story making its rounds.

"Did Hughey's story check out?" Jordan asked. Maybe there was another angle to consider.

"For the most part. Yes. I asked a judge to issue a search warrant for his home, because Rhonda had ketamine in her system as well as alcohol and a prescription opioid," Zach informed.

"Same as Breanna?" Jordan asked.

"It looks like that might be how he gets them to be compliant. He gets them comfortable with him somehow and then slips some powder into their drink when they aren't watching." A picture was beginning to take shape. It wasn't one he liked, but the puzzle pieces fit together and no one could deny it. It was a theory worth considering.

"That could be how he got his victim to the site." Zach sounded like he hadn't slept since yesterday. A pang of guilt struck Jordan, because sleeping with Courtney given him his best night's rest in recent memory. Hell, he hadn't slept that well since the last time they were together.

"I'll keep Courtney at the ranch for a few days if she'll stay. It might help keep her under the radar until talk simmers down," Jordan said.

"She'll want to call in and ask about the case. Tell her I called to check on her and to order her to rest," Zach said.

"She has an independent streak as long as Route 66 and a stubborn streak even longer. I'll see what I can do," Jordan said on a chuckle.

"Do you care about her enough to go the long haul?" Zach asked.

"I haven't figured anything out yet, and especially not my next move," Jordan admitted. "But, yeah, I think so."

"She'd make a fine partner for the right person." Zach wasn't exactly being subtle.

"We're still figuring that part out," Jordan replied.

"She's worth fighting for." Zach left it at that. "One more thing, she cares about you. I saw it before last night, but it's obvious every time she looks at you."

"Thanks, Zach. You know I always appreciate your opinion," Jordan said. "And take care of yourself."

Jordan wanted to do more to pitch in and ease the burden for his cousin. But maybe the best thing he could do right now was take care of Courtney.

If she'd let him, and that was a big if.

She'd always been headstrong. She was also smart, so she wouldn't do anything to put herself or their child in harm's way. She seemed to be coming to terms with the fact that she'd been dealing with her stress in the wrong way.

And she seemed genuinely committed to turning that around for the sake of their child. He had no idea, though, if she was capable of letting him in.

Chapter Sixteen

A day of rest after yesterday seemed like a smart option to Courtney, not for her sake but for the baby's. She'd slept in fits last night. The case was eating at her. It was difficult to walk away completely when the clock was ticking, and especially after an innocent woman had died in Courtney's arms.

For all anyone knew the Jacobstown Hacker may have already made a move on his next victim. Questions swirled about Hughey and what his role truly was. Could he be the person they'd been searching for all along? Could he be the Jacobstown Hacker?

She didn't know him well enough to decide one way or another.

The case wasn't the only thing on her mind as she brushed her teeth. Last night, when she and Jordan made love, something was different between them. Granted, the sex was hotter than ever, but that wasn't what she was talking about. A tide had shifted between them. Their lovemaking had felt more intimate.

Courtney tried to chalk it up to outside factors, like the fact that she'd been through hell and back. That Jordan hadn't gone anywhere. He'd stayed right by her side when she'd needed him the most.

But he lived in Idaho and had willingly left Jacobstown years ago. He had his own demons to deal with, considering he'd walked away from the only place he'd ever known and hadn't looked back. She saw in him what she saw in herself— someone ready to walk away.

Courtney finished brushing her teeth and washed her face. Her mind raced with other thoughts, too.

There was a person she'd been avoiding since returning to town. Amy. Courtney had been dodging Amy's attempts to reach out to her and connect. Courtney felt bad about not returning Amy's calls.

The thought of facing Amy—one of the few people who'd actually known Courtney in Jacobstown—after having a weeklong fling with Jordan didn't sit well.

In the beginning, she didn't think she could trust herself not to slip up. And she'd made a habit of avoiding people she cared about from the past. Wasn't that just an excuse? An excuse to stay miserable in some ways? Because people she cared about who had died didn't get to reconnect with old friends. Why should she?

The people she'd been closest to were gone, all in one fell swoop. A surprising well of tears leaked from her eyes, and this time she didn't rush to wipe them away. Hadn't she been doing that to herself all along? Covering her crying? Wiping away her tears the second they fell while hoping she could erase all that came with them just as easily?

Oh damn. Was that what she'd been doing?

Courtney finished freshening up in the bathroom before making her way into the kitchen. The smell of coffee hit her square in the face as she entered the room, and she had to hold back the nauseous feeling threatening to overpower her.

She located her cell inside her purse, but the battery was low. Not being connected to her work made her chest feel tight. The air in the room thinned, and it suddenly felt hard to breathe.

Thinking about her work made her tense, too. She'd grown used to depending on cell phones and her police radio to stay constantly in touch. Was it any wonder that she usually wanted nothing to do with those things on her days off? And yet not having full access to them was making her a little stir-crazy.

It was most likely because of the gravity of the case and not because of something else, like she feared her job wouldn't be waiting for her after her forced leave.

Jordan wasn't in the kitchen. She figured he wouldn't mind if she helped herself to some yogurt in the fridge. As she walked across the room, she heard faint sounds coming from the office down the hall. It sounded like keystrokes.

It made sense that Jordan would be working. She checked the time. How could it be nine fifteen already? She normally woke up with the sun. It was a habit that came with growing up in ranch country and had stuck well into adulthood.

After talking to Jordan last night, some of the weight she felt like she'd been carrying around for far too long seemed like it had lifted. She plugged her phone into the charger on the wall with every intention of getting enough charge going to check her e-mails and call the counselor.

It was time to learn how to live with what had happened and not run away from it. It was time to deal with her feelings instead of shoving them down deep. It was time to make the fresh start she'd so badly wanted in coming home to Jacobstown.

Maybe it took a surprise pregnancy for Courtney to realize she couldn't live like this anymore. She needed to come to terms with her past. She knew that she had to let it go in order to pave the way for a bright future for her and her child.

She'd had no idea that becoming a mother would make her want to change in almost every way for the better. To take what was good about her and find a way to do more of it. To take what was broken and find a way to fix it.

That was the power of love.

Courtney finished her yogurt and checked the pantry for some table crackers. Salty crackers sounded like they'd calm her stomach, which was doing well so far. The little nugget growing inside her must be hungry. Courtney touched her belly. "I don't know how you got stuck with me, kiddo. I promise to do my best. We'll figure this out together."

She already knew that Jordan Kent was going to be an amazing father. That much was a given. Being a Kent would give their baby everything Courtney never had and everything a child really wanted—a loving family.

Jordan walked into the kitchen, and she dropped her hand.

"Good morning. I didn't realize you were awake," he said.

A moment of hesitation struck. What they'd done last night had changed the course of their relationship. They'd muddied the waters of friendship and co-parenting, and she'd probably made a mess of everything before her child was even in the world.

Jordan walked straight over to her, took her hand and then kissed her with such tenderness it robbed her of breath. She marveled at his ability to walk into a room and make everything better.

"I don't usually sleep so late." They'd kept all kinds of odd hours at the cabin for that blissful week. He wasn't familiar with her normal life routine.

"You needed it." He walked over to the fridge and pulled out a container of food. "Kimberly made a whole mess of food when she heard you were staying at the main house. Does a southwest skillet breakfast sound good to you?"

"Normally, I'd be all over it. Right now, I can make do with yogurt and crackers. I made myself at home." She pointed toward the empty container of yogurt, thinking she probably should've found him and asked first. "I hope you don't mind."

"It would be weird if you didn't make yourself comfortable." He smiled that sexy little smile that had been so good at seducing her. Of course, his tortured look had been pretty damn good at accomplishing the same feat.

"Good. I thought you might be out on the property, and I woke up starving." She picked up her cell phone, which finally had a decent charge.

"Zach says you should leave that thing alone," Jordan stated. "That came straight from your boss."

"I promise that I'm not looking at this thing for

work purposes." She held her hand to her heart like she was taking an oath. "I owe Amy a text at the very least. If she still wants to talk to me."

"She'll like hearing from you." Jordan sounded distracted as he pulled out his phone. "Now that you mention it, I haven't seen her around lately. I probably have a message from her since we've been in contact every day since I've been home. Hold on while I check."

A sinking feeling hit Courtney in the pit of her stomach as he stared at his screen, scrolling through message after message.

He looked up at her and shook his head.

JORDAN CHECKED HIS phone again. There was nothing from Amy. It was most likely the fact that everyone, including him, was on high alert, but he had a bad feeling.

"I tried texting her a minute ago. She didn't respond. She could be mad at me and I'd deserve it." Courtney held out her cell.

"That's not like her." If Amy wasn't returning Courtney's text, it could mean that she was busy. Or…

His mind dived to darker places—places he couldn't allow himself to stay for long or he'd drive himself crazy. "I'm sure Zach's heard from her. We can clear this up with a phone call. There's no reason to panic."

Jordan pulled up Zach's name and made the call.

"What's up, Jordan?" Zach asked by way of answer. His voice gave away how tired he must be.

"Is Amy around? She's not answering her cell, and I have a quick question for her." He didn't want Zach to worry. Jordan told himself that he was being overly cautious.

"No. In fact, I haven't seen her. Let me ask Ellen. My sister has probably already shown up to volunteer today. Hold on." Jordan could hear his cousin shout to his secretary even though his mouth was away from the receiver.

Jordan looked at Courtney, who was fiddling with the spoon in her hand. She looked up at him with so much worry in her beautiful brown eyes.

Zach returned to the call. "No one has seen her. I'm trying to think the last time I did. It's been a full day, which has me concerned."

"I'll reach out to Amber and Isaac. We can see if they've heard anything," Jordan immediately offered.

"Let me know what they say. In the meantime, I'll give her a call and let her know we're looking for her. I'm sure everything's fine, but I'm glad you called to check." There was no conviction in those first four words.

"Okay then. Let's all get busy." Jordan figured that between Amber and Isaac, someone had seen or spoken to Amy. His first call was to his sister.

She picked up on the first ring. "Hey, Jordan. How are you?"

"I'm good. I'm calling about Amy. Do you know where she is?" He got right to the point.

"Um, hmm. Good question. Let's see. We were supposed to go to the VFW together to drop off a baked goods. And then news spread about what happened last night, so we canceled." She paused a beat. "Hold on. There was so much confusion yesterday, now that I think about it, I'm not even sure that I talked to her. *Everyone* was calling and trying to find out what was going on, and I assumed she had, too."

"So, you didn't talk to her?" Jordan looked at Courtney.

"Now that I really think about it, no. Patsy Blair was coordinating the annual baked goods event, and I must've talked to her half a dozen times. But I actually don't remember having a conversation with Amy now that you mention it. Why? What's going on?" Concern caused her voice to raise a few octaves.

"I hope nothing. She and Isaac are still dating, right?" he asked.

"You know about that?" Amber sounded shocked.

"Pretty much everyone does at this point. They've been on and off for how many years now?" he asked.

"That's fair," Amber said quickly. And then added, "Let me know what you hear from him, okay?"

"Will do, sis." Zach and Amber spoke to Amy on a daily basis, so Jordan wasn't one bit thrilled about what he was hearing. His next call was to Isaac, who answered immediately.

"How can I help you, Jordan?" They'd long ago dispensed with formalities.

"You haven't seen Amy around, have you?" Jordan held his breath waiting for the answer.

"As a matter of fact, no, I haven't. I've been working double shifts like everybody else." Isaac and the other security personnel had volunteered their time off in order to take extra shifts. Everyone had been on heightened alert since the delivery the other morning. "Why?"

Jordan figured he might as well tell Isaac. "No one has seen or heard from her in the last twenty-four hours."

"Well, then, I request permission to abandon my post and look for her," Isaac said without missing a beat. "Frederick's here and can keep watch on the gate."

"Absolutely. Brief the others on the situation. I'll call Lone Star Lonnie personally." Lonnie was like family and he needed to know what was going on.

Breanna's murder was out there somewhere. Rhonda had been murdered in the field. A coldblooded killer was out there somewhere. And Amy was MIA.

Dammit. Dammit. Dammit.

"I'll report back the minute I hear from her," Isaac said.

"Thank you." He ended the call and fired off a text to his siblings. A rush of adrenaline blasted Jordan, and all his senses heightened.

One glance at Courtney, and he saw that she was already on the phone.

"It doesn't hurt to ask around," she said.

Within a few minutes, it was clear that Amy hadn't been seen or heard from in at least the past twenty-four hours. A mix of anger and fear rushed Jordan. "We should check her house just to be certain she's not asleep."

"I'm ready when you are." Courtney wasted no time putting on her boots from work and then her coat.

Jordan was ready, and the two of them were out the door in a matter of minutes. Zach called before they left Kent property.

"I'm at Amy's place and she's not here. Her cat's food bowl is empty, and so is the water," Zach said.

She always left food for her cat. She said Mr. Nibbles liked to snack all day. But the water was the most concerning.

Amy would never allow that bowl to go dry.

So where was she?

Chapter Seventeen

The news about Amy spread like wildfire through the community within the hour. Jordan was certain his cousin had touched just about every life in Jacobstown with her generosity and kind spirit. She could also be feisty and wild, so there was a slight hope that she was off doing something fun and had lost track of time.

She knew Isaac was working extra shifts over the next few days. It would also be like Amy, on a whim, to drive to Fort Worth or a nearby town in order to deliver those cookies meant for the VFW. She wouldn't have wanted them to go to waste and might figure everyone in town was too preoccupied with criminal activity to be able to enjoy them.

"Her cell could've run out of battery," Courtney offered as they navigated the streets of town, searching for signs of Amy.

"That sounds like her," Jordan said, but there was no energy in those words.

"We'll find her," she promised, but that was one they both knew she couldn't keep.

"If I spent more time here, I'd know more about her habits," Jordan said. "I've been thinking about moving here full-time. I want to be closer to you and the baby."

"You said you could never see yourself living here again." Her words were true enough.

"Things have changed. I don't want to be a part-time dad who sees his kid summers and holidays," he said.

"Oh." Why did she sound so deflated?

"I thought you'd be happy about this news," he admitted.

"If you come here because of a child and not for yourself, do you think you'll resent not being able to live the life you want?" It was a fair question and one that deserved an answer.

Before he could tell her that *was* the life he wanted, his cell phone interrupted them. He pulled to the side of the road and parked.

"Hey, Zach. What's going on?" he asked his cousin.

"We just picked up Reggie Barstock. I thought you should know he's in custody," Zach informed.

"What kind of vehicle was he driving?" Courtney immediately asked.

"A white sedan," Zach supplied.

Damn. It wasn't a pickup.

"And he's not talking. He lawyered up almost immediately, but we do have his vehicle and probable cause to take it apart since he tried to outrun us. We also got a tip on the pickup. Posting the picture online brought out a few folks from Bexford. They all said the same thing. A guy by the name of Jason Millipede owns a truck that matches the picture. When they were asked to describe it, they described the same pickup you saw at the murder scene last night."

"That name sounds familiar," Courtney said. "Why do I know it?"

"Good question." Zach shrugged. "Any thoughts?"

She shook her head. "It's not coming to me. I need to think some more."

"Did you get any additional information on the guy?" Jordan asked Zach. "Did you ask about any injuries?"

"Yeah. It turns out the guy injured his ankle as a kid. His neighbors haven't seen him in a few days, but that's no surprise. They said he keeps odd hours. They all said he's quiet. I got the name of his aunt and have been trying to get in contact with her. Other than that, he has no other family around. He's been living with his aunt since he was little," Zach said.

"Did anyone have any ideas on where he might be?" Courtney shot a glance at Jordan, who was taking all this information in and trying his level best to fit the puzzle pieces together.

"No. He hasn't turned up in a few days," Zach answered.

"What about his address?" Courtney snapped into full deputy mode.

Zach hesitated. "I think the best thing the two of you can do is keep searching for Amy. This is a courtesy call to let you know your tip about The Mart is panning out and could lead to something big. I want you as far away from this guy as possible."

"Zach—"

"I'm serious, Courtney." There was a finality to Zach's tone that she seemed to know better than to argue with.

"Thanks for the information, Zach. I'm grateful to be in the loop," she finally said on a sharp sigh.

"Lopez is on his way to investigate in Bexford. He has the case." Zach softened his tone when he said, "Right now, let's go out there, find Amy and bring her home."

"I KNOW HE said we shouldn't investigate in Bexford, but I need to talk to this guy's neighbors myself and possibly the aunt if we can locate her. Please, Jordan. It might mean the difference between finding Amy in time." Courtney could only pray her plea would work.

"Putting you in jeopardy isn't going to help anyone. We know this guy likes the ranch. Maybe we should head there instead." Jordan had a point.

"I don't know. I feel like Zach is holding back, and he should. I'm not technically part of this investigation anymore." A thought kept trying to break through. "This guy's name seems familiar, but I can't for the life of me figure out why."

"Google him and see what you come up with." Jordan motioned toward the cell in her hand.

Courtney performed the search. "There's no information here."

"If he's from the area, it makes sense that he'd be familiar with the ranch." Jordan thumped the steering wheel as he navigated onto the road and performed a U-turn toward his home.

Jordan's cell buzzed. "Will you check that for me while I drive?"

Courtney picked up his phone. "It's a text from Zach. He said Robert at the corner store said he saw Amy yesterday afternoon at lunch."

"I'm guessing Zach is also telling us to go home and wait for word," Jordan said.

"No. He didn't."

This time, Jordan's cell rang.

Courtney checked the screen. "It's your sister."

"I'll answer it on speaker." He pushed a button on his steering wheel, and two notes sounded.

"Jordan?" Amber's voice came through clearly.

"I'm driving and Courtney is with me—"

"Is it true? Is Amy missing?" Amber's voice was loaded with panic.

"I'm afraid so," Jordan stated.

"I just talked to Isaac. He said the two of them were supposed to meet up at his place later tonight. I told him to give us a call if he sees her, but…"

"Right now, it's important to stay positive," Jordan said. "Amy needs us to think with a clear head."

"You're right." Amber sniffed, and it was easy to tell that she'd been crying.

"Do you remember her mentioning a guy by the name of Jason Millipede?" Courtney interjected. "His name sounds familiar, but I can't place him."

"I can," Amber said plainly. "We met him the summer after seventh grade at Camp Pine Needles."

"Oh, right. I remember you and Amy talking about that." Courtney's father had refused to let her go, even though she promised to work in order to earn the money. He'd thought camp was frivolous spending, but this place accepted every kid, even the ones who worked in order to supplement the fees.

Amber gasped. "It was so long ago. I never really thought about it before. He shattered his ankle when a barrel rolled down the hill on him. It was awful. Gruesome. He was in so much pain. I guess he'd been out in the wooded area where he wasn't supposed to go when it happened. Some older boys tied him to a tree and rolled a heavy metal barrel down the hill aimed at him. They took off and just left him there. Amy found him first and ran to get help. I ran into her when she was on her way, so I went with her. The camp counselors never figured out who rolled that barrel at him. He never would say but he sure looked at Amy like she was some kind of savior. He'd managed to scoot around the side of the tree before the metal barrel hit more of him." She grunted as though in disgust. "I can't believe anyone would do that to another human being. I know the kid was considered weird, and I'm ashamed to admit it but I thought so, too, but he didn't deserve to be treated that way."

Courtney didn't need to ask the next question, but she did anyway. "It was his left ankle, wasn't it?"

"I guess. I mean, I never really paid attention to which one until we started talking about it just now," Amber stated. "He never even crossed my mind until I heard his name again. We were kids back then. It's been more than thirteen years. I do remember him seeming kind of fixated on Amy, though"

"Call Zach and tell him everything you just told me," Courtney instructed. "And then meet us at the main house."

Jordan barely waited for the call to end before he asked, "If Amy helped this guy, wouldn't that be a good thing?"

"It could be. It's possible that he developed a fixation like Amber said. Maybe she was the only girl who'd ever been nice to him. I'd like to get more information about his aunt. There's just too much we don't know to make a determination," she said. "Anything we say right now is just guessing without concrete information to go on. It can lead us down the wrong path. It's best to keep an open mind right now and follow the evidence."

Jordan kept his gaze on the stretch of road in front of them. His phone was going off like a pinball machine. "Do you mind taking a look and letting me know if anything important comes through?"

She picked up his cell and saw the number of texts going into the double digits. She skimmed them, but they were mostly from his family, asking if there was any new information on Amy.

"Looks like Amber put out word for everyone to come to the main house," she said. She scanned a few more before the one from Zach came. "This one looks important. It's from your cousin. Amy's car was found abandoned at the mouth of Hermosa Creek."

"That's three miles from her house." He braked hard enough for Courtney to feel it. She put her hand up against the dashboard to steady herself.

"Sorry about that," he said, and she could hear the frustration for the situation in his tone.

"Zach's already there. He won't want us to show up," she said. The cell buzzed again. "In fact, he just warned against it."

"It's the last place we know she was. Maybe she's around that area," he said.

"He wouldn't keep her near her car. That's too obvious." She pounded the dash with the flat of her palm. "Zach wouldn't tell us if there'd been any pickup sightings."

"Maybe the guy's aware of the pictures of his pickup being distributed," Jordan said. "Or one of his neighbors tipped him off about law enforcement looking for him."

"I hope not. That wouldn't be good for Amy," she replied.

"Because?"

"If he truly is fixated on her, then she's his grand prize. The others might've been lead ups or he could've killed to try to impress Amy. This kind of monster isn't playing with a full deck. He could have had some interaction with her that made him feel rejected—"

"Amy has one of the best hearts of anyone I know. She helps everyone. Her path may have crossed with his while she was doing something for others. She helps serve meals to homeless people. She's the first to take food to the elderly or anyone who is sick and can't do for themselves. If this bastard harms a hair on her head…" Jordan tightened his grip on the steering wheel.

"We'll find her, Jordan." It was a promise she prayed she'd be able to keep.

Chapter Eighteen

"Let's break into search parties. There's a good chance he'll take her somewhere on the property," Courtney said to the Kent family who'd assembled in the main house. "Women with young children might want to stay in the main house together with locked doors. Jordan and I will be Team One."

Courtney divided the rest of the Kents into two-person teams.

She turned to Leah and Amber, who were standing at the granite island. "Set the alarm while we're gone. Okay?"

"I'm going," Leah stated. As a former Fort Worth detective, no one could argue she had the skillset to track a criminal.

"You can team up with Rylan," Jordan said. "He might be hiding her close to the house. Do you want to start there?"

Leah nodded as Amber texted Rylan to meet Leah.

"Do you mind keeping things stabilized here?" Jordan asked his sister.

"Not if you think this is where I'll do the most good." Amber could keep the situation stabilized at the main house.

Courtney looked at Amber. "Every set? You're okay with this?"

"I'll hold down the fort here and keep watch around the house," she said.

"Thank you." Walking outside, Courtney was blasted with a hit of cold air. The temperature had dropped a good fifteen degrees in the last hour, and it was becoming bitterly cold.

Zach was already out with Isaac, who'd been searching the property ever since he found out his girlfriend was missing.

When she and Jordan had been walking a solid half hour, they ran into Zach.

"What the hell are you doing out here?" Zach's question was laser-focused on Courtney. "I told you to stay out of the search."

"I'm not alone," she defended. "We need all hands on deck, Zach. I want to help find your sister." Her voice was pleading now. "I care about what happens to her."

Zach blew out a sharp breath and conceded with a warning look.

"What did you find out about Barstock?" Jordan asked his cousin as Isaac and Courtney paired up on the perimeter of the area. She stayed close enough to listen.

"We know he's not involved in Amy's disappearance, but we did find incriminating evidence in his vehicle. We threatened him with murder charges, and it didn't take long for him to start naming names and asking for immunity. He's been slipping in and out of town because he's involved with a human-trafficking ring," Zach informed. "We have enough to lock him away for a very long time. He won't get out until he's too old to hurt anyone else."

At least one scumbag was going to jail. Hughey couldn't be responsible for Amy's disappearance because he'd been with Rhonda last night. Well, it didn't completely rule him out if Amy had gone missing more than twenty-four hours ago, but it made him less likely to be a suspect.

It really was down to Jason.

Unfortunately, nothing they knew about him could tip them off to where he might've taken Amy.

Her thoughts shifted to Jordan. In every instance, he'd been there for her. He never made excuses or disappeared when life got tough. Instead, he was figuring out how to move back to Jacobstown in order to be the best father to their child.

Even when she'd tried to push him away early on, he'd stood his ground and been there when she needed him. He was her true north, and she'd been too scared to let herself acknowledge it before now.

She'd been a fool. He'd been trying to tell her that he cared about her, and she'd done nothing but run the opposite way. Granted, she had some work to do when it came to trusting others. But Jordan Kent was the most trustworthy, true-to-his-word person she'd ever met.

As soon as Amy was home safe, Courtney planned to have a conversation with Jordan about her growing feelings for him.

A shiver raced down her spine being out here and searching for someone she'd been so close to. There was no way in hell she planned to let Amy down.

A gunshot caused everyone to scatter in order to find cover behind trees. Courtney drew her weapon, and she heard Zach and Isaac do the same.

"Everyone okay?" came Zach's hushed voice.

"I'm good," Isaac responded first.

"Same," came from Jordan.

Before Courtney could speak, she took a blow to the back of the head.

JORDAN LISTENED FOR the sound of Courtney's voice. There was no way this jerk got to her while they were all together. Right? The shotgun blast had sounded from farther away. Jordan's pulse jacked up as he moved stealthily along the tree line toward Zach.

"We'll cover more ground if we split up," he said to his cousin, his gaze searching for Courtney.

"There might be more than one person involved," Zach warned, and he seemed to catch on to the panic growing inside Jordan.

"I'll keep my eyes peeled." His pulse jackhammered his ribs when he couldn't locate Courtney. "Where is she?"

Isaac was beside them in the next beat. He was easy to hear coming. Jordan had no plans to give the Hacker warning or let him know what hit him. Jordan figured the four of them had been making too much noise and that had tipped the guy off.

Both Zach and Isaac surveyed the area.

"Courtney," Jordan called her name even though a lead ball sank to the pit of his stomach.

A moment of panic struck that the shotgun blast was the result of Amy being shot. But he talked himself out of that unproductive thinking. If this guy stayed true to form, she was tucked somewhere passed out on ketamine. The idea wasn't exactly comforting, but it was better than the alternative…

Zach cursed and Isaac tried to put his fist through a tree trunk.

"I have to find her. We'll cover more ground if we split up," Jordan said.

A reluctant nod came from Zach. "Stay in constant contact."

"Will do." As Jordan broke off from the now-trio, he realized the only thing that mattered was bringing Courtney and Amy home. Amy was family, and he would do anything for her. And so was Courtney. She was going to be his family now, too. Somewhere in his heart, he'd realized it a long time ago. Letting his brain catch up was another issue. But it had. And he loved her.

What more could he offer than that? What else mattered?

Jordan knew this part of the property like the back of his hand, and he knew exactly where Rushing Creek wound through the trees. The creek was at its widest half a mile up, so he headed there figuring that would give Jason enough space to work with now that he had two victims. Had that been his plan all along?

Courtney wouldn't have gone down without a fight or making a sound, which meant she'd been surprised. Frustration was a punch in the solar plexus. Taking in air hurt.

He couldn't allow himself to doubt that she was alive. This jerk was rubbing their noses in his ability to come and go as he pleased, taking whatever he wanted. Well, this was Kent property, and Jason Millipede didn't belong there.

It was time for Jordan to take his rightful place

alongside his brothers and sister. It was time to put the past behind him and move on with his life. It was time to look to his future—a future with Courtney, if she'd have him.

For several minutes, Jordan moved through the trees toward the small clearing. He could hear his heartbeat in his ears, thrumming at a frantic clip.

PAIN SHOT THROUGH Courtney's head as she tried to open her eyes. It felt like her head might explode. What the hell had happened?

And then it all came rushing back to her. Jason Millipede had whacked her in the back of the head with a blunt object. She was on Kent property in the woods. She tried to scream but couldn't. There was something covering her mouth. Courtney forced her eyes open and was startled to find a pair of blue eyes staring back at her.

It took a second to register those frightened eyes belonged to Amy.

Relief that she was alive washed over Courtney. Her next thought was about Jordan. If something happened to Amy, he would be devastated. Courtney strained to get a better look and could see that Amy's mouth was covered with clear tape.

She tried to move, but her hands were tied behind her back. Pain registered with movement. Courtney assessed that she was lying on her side in some type of shallow grave. Creepy-crawlies ran up her back at the thought of being buried alive.

But that wasn't the death Jason Millipede wanted for them.

On closer appraisal, Amy seemed…*off.* Courtney remembered the ketamine that had been used on the other victims. Maybe he hadn't planned for Amy to be alive this long.

There was something on top of them, and from what Courtney could gather it was a branch. Someone would have to fall into the grave with them in order to realize it was there.

Was this what he did? Stored his victims in a freshly dug grave. Drugged them so they were compliant. And then once he was ready and had them in position…

Another icy chill gripped her spine.

The ground was hard and cold. Courtney thought about the little nugget growing inside her. She became more resolved to stay alive.

Trying to talk was pretty much impossible. She tried to move her legs and feet. They were bound together at her ankles.

Movement made her brain hurt.

She heard footsteps and froze. She listened. Jordan would be looking for her, as would Zach and Isaac. The four of them had been on the hunt for Amy, and the others wouldn't give up. If anything, the search would intensify.

Courtney knew for certain if Jason took them to another spot, it would be even more difficult to escape. So, when the branch moved and she saw his face, she waited until he got close enough, and then she unleashed hell.

Amy seemed to catch on and she rolled onto her back and thrust her feet toward Jason, connecting with his chest.

He made an animal-like growl before he seemed to realize he'd made a mistake. Courtney figured it was now or never, so she kicked with everything she had and knocked him back a couple of steps. Blood squirted from his nose. She rolled onto her side and scrambled to get to her feet while Amy did the same.

Jason disappeared from view, and she realized he'd come back with something to knock out her and Amy or kill them this time.

She scooted toward Amy and motioned for her to go back to back. Tape wasn't hard to tear once a small tear was made. Courtney struggled with it for a few precious seconds before she was able to dig her nail hard enough to rip the tape on Amy's wrists. Amy immediately ripped off their mouth tape and started to work on Courtney.

"No, go. Get out of there. Undo your ankles and go get help. Jordan, Zach and Isaac are out here somewhere. Find them and bring them back." Courtney used her stern law enforcement voice. It was authoritative, and people instinctively knew she meant business.

Amy hesitated.

"Go. The second you're safely away from here, I'll start screaming to draw attention," she urged.

"I can't leave you like this. We can fight him together. We're stronger together." Amy went to work on Courtney's wrists. "I'm not as fast as you are, but I'll get it."

True to her word, she worked the tape until Courtney's hands were free. She immediately removed the tape from her ankles with Amy's help.

The two locked arms and set out to run on wobbly legs.

"Not so fast." Jason's voice was shrill. They heard the snick of a bullet being engaged in a chamber.

"On three, we need to shout as loud as we can and dive for the tree," Courtney whispered. She'd only been in there a short time, and still her legs and arms hurt. She could only imagine how painful it must be for Amy right then.

"Let's do this," came the hushed response.

"One. Two. Three." Courtney held on to Amy as they ran behind a tree, screaming as loud as their voices would carry.

"I said stop," Jason's agitated voice demanded.

When they didn't, he fired a shot.

Courtney pulled Amy to the ground. The pair huddled together as they continued to shout for help.

"How could you do this to me, Amy?" Jason shouted. "I thought you were special. You're just a tramp like the others. My aunt warned me about girls like you, and she was right. You pretend to be nice, but really all you want to do is hurt me like the others did. I did everything to show you how strong I am now. Everything I accomplished was to impress you. Instead, you look at me like I'm the one who's evil. You fight me and try to run. This is how you repay me?"

"Breanna deserved to live," Amy said quietly. "Hurting someone else to prove you're somebody doesn't make you look stronger. It makes you pathetic."

There was something almost pitiful about Jason.

But he was a coldblooded killer, and her sympathy stopped right there.

JORDAN HEARD THE SCREAMS. He also heard the shot. And then there was nothing but quiet.

Pain shot through his calves and his thighs as he pushed his legs harder. All he could think about was seeing Courtney and Amy alive again. He let that thought motivate him to run when his lungs might explode from needing air.

He was too close to lose her. So he pushed harder. And then he slowed his pace to a catlike crawl. He stalked closer toward where the noise had been.

Another shot fired, and someone screamed.

It was near pitch-black outside, but his eyes had adjusted to the dark long ago. His hands were frozen, so he rubbed them together as he neared the direction of the gunfire. He could only hope it was Courtney's gun and she was in control of it.

When he happened upon the scene, he realized Jason had the gun.

Neither Courtney nor Amy was anywhere to be seen.

He neared the lone gunman with stealthy precision. And then Jordan saw Jason put the gun to his own head.

"Oh no you don't, bastard," Jordan said as he tackled Jason from behind in time to knock his hand away from his head in time. Blood squirted, but Jordan knocked Jason onto his stomach on the hard ground. He went to work stemming the flow of blood. "You don't get to take the easy way out and die. You're going to spend the rest of your long life behind bars, where you belong."

Zach and Isaac showed up at almost exactly the same time.

"We need an EMT and zip cuffs," Jordan said to Zach.

"I have a pair right here. EMT is on the way."

Zach dug his knee into the perp's back as Amy and Courtney rushed over.

"Is everyone okay?" Jordan was on his feet in half a second and by Courtney's side.

Isaac and Amy embraced a second later.

"We made it," Courtney said. "We survived."

Jordan pulled her into an embrace, where she stayed. It didn't take long for the scene to bustle with activity.

Amy gave her statement   she'd stopped to help a stranded motorist and had been attacked from behind before something was shoved into her mouth.

Jordan couldn't leave Courtney's side if he'd wanted to. He'd almost lost her once, and when all this settled down, he had something to say to her.

It took a solid hour for her to be cleared from the scene. A deputy had brought over a warm blanket. Another was given to Amy as the Jacobstown Hacker was being hauled off in handcuffs.

Jordan turned to Courtney and was pretty sure he saw nothing but love in her eyes when she looked at him. "There's no rush for our relationship to magically work out. But I know what's in your heart, and I happen to love you with all of mine. I want you to know that I'm willing to wait as long as you need to be able to say the words back. I love you, Courtney."

"I don't want to wait to tell you how I feel, Jordan. Life is uncertain and can be taken away in a second. I know that I have work to do and I'm far from perfect, but I love you in a perfect way. I want to have a family with you." She touched her stomach. "And this child will be the luckiest kid on earth to be surrounded by so much love."

He kissed her. "I have a real shock for you. I want you to be my wife."

"Then all that's left for me to say is yes. I'll marry you, Jordan. I'm ready to spend the rest of my life with you. You are the only person I've ever truly trusted with my heart. The only person I can ever see myself loving. It's always been you—even before the tragedy that left me broken. With you, I feel like I've found home, a *real* home, and not just a place to lay my head at night, because up until you that's all I've ever done."

"Good. Because I'm done running away. I want to run to you and to our family. Because I can't imagine loving anyone more than I love you. I don't care where you want to settle down, because you're my home." Jordan wrapped his arms around the woman who would be his bride and pressed his lips to hers. "I almost lost you tonight. I never want to have that feeling again."

And he kissed her. His love. His Courtney. His home.

Epilogue

"Good morning, Mrs. Farmer," Courtney said to her former neighbor.

"You're glowing," Mrs. Farmer said as she put both hands on Courtney's very round, very pregnant belly after greeting her at the door while Sassy jumped and barked around Courtney's ankles. The gold band on Courtney's left hand sparkled against the sunlight.

"She'll be here in a week or two. Maybe sooner from the way I feel." Courtney handed over a basket filled with fresh fruit and a few muffins. It had become their favorite Monday morning meal.

"Where's Amy today?" Mrs. Farmer asked, ushering Courtney through the door and to the kitchen table after Courtney picked up Sassy and gave her snuggles.

"She and Isaac decided to take a trip out of the blue. Just the two of them," Courtney said with a smile. "I wouldn't be surprised if she came back married."

Mrs. Farmer burst out laughing. "Sounds like something Amy would do. Those two deserve all the happiness in the world." She shook her index finger in the air. "And so do you. You deserve that gorgeous man you married."

Courtney's cheeks flushed at the compliment.

"Amy said to tell you she'll see you next week and that I should give you a big hug for her." Courtney embraced the woman who'd become family. "Jordan sends his love."

"I'm surprised he let you out of his sight," Mrs. Farmer teased.

"He is definitely a husband on baby watch. But I think he also knows that I wouldn't miss our breakfasts for the world." A cramp struck, and her belly felt like it contracted, reminding her that she wouldn't be waiting too much longer to meet her daughter.

Her daughter. Courtney's chest filled with so much love it felt like she might burst every time she thought about her little girl. She credited her sessions with Sara Winters for helping her break down her walls and enjoy all the love that surrounded her now. She still had work to do and it would take time, but she looked to the future with hope for the first time. Hope was a beautiful thing. Happiness was even better.

"I squeezed fresh juice this morning." Mrs. Farmer beamed.

"Well, we better eat before this baby decides to come and interrupt our meal," Courtney teased.

Mrs. Farmer caught her gaze. "Did you make a decision about going back to work after the baby's born?"

Courtney glanced down and touched her stomach. "I have a feeling that I have my work cut out for me right here. I don't want to miss a minute of her day."

"You'll never regret being home with your child," Mrs. Farmer agreed. "Jenny and Hanson are bringing my Ellie bell later this fall."

Her son-in-law's job had moved the family to Europe three years ago. They'd offered to move back when Mr. Farmer passed away, but Mrs. Farmer wouldn't have it. She'd said she wanted them to live their lives. She wasn't ready to leave Jacobstown to join them because she felt closer to her husband here.

The warmth in Mrs. Farmer's voice when she spoke about her family caused a few tears to fall from Courtney's eyes.

There were no better words than love, family and home. Having all three made Courtney feel like the luckiest person in the world.

* * * * *

Don't miss the previous books in
USA TODAY bestselling author Barb Han's
Rushing Creek Crime Spree miniseries:

Cornered at Christmas
Ransom at Christmas
Ambushed at Christmas
What She Did
What She Knew

Available now from Harlequin Intrigue!

After very little sleep and an early call from his father the next
morning, Brick dressed in his uniform and drove down to the law
enforcement building. He was hoping that this would be the day
that his father, Marshal Hud Savage, told him he would finally be
on active duty. He couldn't wait to get his teeth into something, a
real investigation. After finding that woman last night, he wanted
more than anything to be the one to get her justice.

"Come in and close the door," his father said before motioning
him into a chair across from his desk.

"Is this about the woman I encountered last night?" he asked
as he removed his Stetson and dropped into a chair across from
his father. He'd stayed at the hospital until the doctor had sent him
home. When he called this morning, he'd been told that the woman
appeared to be in a catatonic state and was unresponsive.

"We have a name on your Jane Doe," his father said now.
"Natalie Berkshire."

Brick frowned. The name sounded vaguely familiar. But that
wasn't what surprised him. "Already? Her fingerprints?"

Hud nodded and slid a copy of the *Billings Gazette* toward him.
He picked it up and saw the headline sprawled across the front
page, "Alleged Infant Killer Released for Lack of Evidence." The
newspaper was two weeks old.

Brick felt a jolt rock him back in his chair. "She's that woman?" He couldn't help his shock. He thought of the terrified woman who'd crossed in front of his truck last night. She was nothing like the woman he remembered seeing on television coming out of the law enforcement building in Billings after being released.

"I don't know what to say." Nor did he know what to think. The woman he'd found had definitely been victimized. He thought he'd saved her. He'd been hell-bent on getting her justice. With his Stetson balanced on his knee, he raked his fingers through his hair.

"I'm trying to make sense of this, as well," his father said. "Since her release, more evidence had come out in former cases. She's now wanted for questioning in more deaths of patients who'd been under her care from not just Montana. Apparently, the moment she was released, she disappeared. Billings PD checked her apartment. It appeared that she'd left in a hurry and hasn't been seen since."

"Until last night when she stumbled in front of my pickup," Brick said. "You think she's been held captive all this time?"

"Looks that way," Hud said. "We found her older-model sedan parked behind the convenience store down on Highway 191. We're assuming she'd stopped for gas. The attendant who was on duty recognized her from a photo. She remembered seeing Natalie at the gas pumps and thinking she looked familiar but couldn't place her at the time. The attendant said a large motor home pulled in and she lost sight of her and didn't see her again."

"When was this?" Brick asked.

"Two weeks ago. Both the back seat and the trunk of her car were full of her belongings."

"So she was running away when she was abducted." Brick couldn't really blame her. "After all the bad publicity, I can see where she couldn't stay in Billings. But taking off like that makes her either look guilty—or scared."

"Or both."

Don't miss
Double Action Deputy *by B.J. Daniels,*
available July 2020 wherever
Harlequin Intrigue books and ebooks are sold.

Harlequin.com

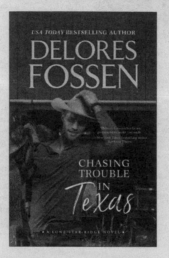